Cactus in a Calabash

MANYI ANABOR has a deep-rooted passion for the protection of children from sexual abuse and sexual exploitation.

Her debut poetry collection, *Storm not Strong Enough*, was published in 2017. *Cactus in a Calabash* is her first book, published in 2019.

Cactus in a Calabash

BY

Manyi Anabor

For My Children

'I am not a writer.

I just have a story to tell.'

MANYI ANABOR

The School Term

KEBI HATED BEING LATE and it was already three-forty. Her psychotherapy session was scheduled for four o'clock and despite sprinting to the bus stop after completing her shift at the sexual health clinic, she narrowly missed the 326 bus. A bit anxious, she looked up and saw that the next bus would arrive in six minutes. In his last email, the therapist said his office building was located next to Canal Bank which Kebi went past every day on her commute to work. It was probably a twenty-minute walk away. As she considered walking there instead of waiting for the bus, she realised she might need to run all the way, in order to get there on time. But she was already sweaty from her brief sprint to the bus stop and did not want to arrive at her first ever therapy session sweating, so she decided to wait for the bus. Just then, she spotted the 18 bus coming up in the stream of heavy traffic and was relieved to find out it went towards Canal Bank. When it finally pulled up, she sat at the front seat so she would see the road ahead and not miss her stop. As she dabbed her sweaty forehead with a handkerchief, she thought, *I can't believe I'm actually going to therapy.*

If her family back in Cameroon heard she was going to therapy, they would certainly be shocked; and if they found out why she was going, most of them would worry but say nothing while a minority few would reach out by phone call or text message. And even if they did, Kebi would make it seem as if her reason for going to therapy was trivial so she would not have to talk about it. Unfortunately, this was what she was used to while growing up in her family home in Cameroon where she lived with her immediate and extended family, wherein issues were either completely swept under the rug or partially addressed.

Her mom, widely referred to as Mama, was quiet and deferential while Papa was authoritarian and overly protective not only of his own children but of the thirty-plus relatives who had moved into his home over the years. In their culture, it was common for extended family members to live together in the same household; a man's nephews and nieces were considered his children and his cousins were considered his brothers and sisters. Fortunately, Papa's house had more than enough room for extended family so they all lived together; aunts and uncles, cousins and grandparents, house girls and house boys. Papa's extensive main house which was bordered by a white bricked fence and tall coconut trees contained five bedrooms and four bathrooms with four additional en-suite bedrooms at the boys' quarters. There were two large living rooms – one for family and the other for guests, and a spacious dining room which despite comfortably seating eight people, was only regularly used by Papa for his evening meals.

Papa was a self-employed barrister and solicitor who worked at his busy law firm six days a week. He also liked to *eat with the children* but by the time he came home from work every night, they had already dined so they politely declined whenever he asked them to join him at the table. However, eight year old Kebi never shied away from joining him for her second dinner; for not only did Papa get huge quantities of food which he was unable to finish but his meals were much tastier. Papa loved the fact that Kebi always agreed to join him for dinner. While they dined, if he saw that her plate was getting empty, he added more food to it especially if it was one of her favourite meals (*eru*, *country njama njama* or *bush meat pepper soup*), then he sat back and watched her eat with a smile on his face.

Unbeknownst to Papa and everyone else, the reason why Kebi joined him for dinner was because she was being sexually abused by their house boy, George. He abused her twice a day; after school and at night when everyone was asleep. However, if he found her alone at any other time, he seized the opportunity to abuse her again. As a result, she always hung around older relatives and offered to help them with lengthy tasks such as peeling *egusi*, folding mounds of laundry or better still, she sat with them to eat. She knew if she appeared to be busy with an older relative, George was less likely to call for her.

For the same reason, Kebi hated the school term because most of her relatives returned to boarding school and out of town universities leaving her and her brothers, Ebot (six) and Junior (three) at home with

4

George, who maltreated them and made Kebi cook all their meals despite the fact that she did not know how to cook. And if the food turned out poorly-cooked, he beat her for *trying to poison everybody*.

One afternoon after school, whilst seated at the backyard waiting for the rice she was cooking to get ready, George asked if she had added salt to the rice. Although she had not, she said she had so he would not beat her. Moments later, she asked (him) for permission to go to the toilet so she would sneak into the kitchen and add salt to the rice. As usual, he gave her ten seconds. She dashed into the main house and tiptoed to the kitchen where she quickly sprinkled a handful of salt over the rice and ran back out as he counted to ten. Later on, he went in and tasted the rice and calmly asked her to come and explain what she had done to make it taste so salty. Before she could open her mouth, his fist landed on her jaw and her head smashed into the kitchen sink. As she began to apologise, he pushed her down and repeatedly kicked her in the stomach – he did this often. She curled up and raised her knees to her chest to stop him from kicking her stomach but he kicked her legs and arms while shouting at her to straighten out her legs. She tried hard not to cry because she, Ebot and Junior were prohibited from crying during beatings. George seemed more enraged that she was blocking his kicks from reaching her stomach so he kicked harder until she was under the kitchen sink at which point she gave in and burst into tears. Infuriated by her crying, he dragged her out from underneath the sink and with his face only inches away from hers, he shouted.

"Did I not say you should not cry?"

She took a deep breath and did her best to stop crying but continued panting.

He slapped her across the face and shouted.

"I have warned you... go and wait for me in the toilet," and with all his might he kicked her towards the door.

Despite the intense pain she felt, she scrambled on all fours into the *brown toilet* which was right next to the kitchen - he always asked her to wait for him there so he could come in and rub his penis against her inner thighs as punishment. Although she never understood how rubbing his penis on her thighs was a form of punishment (because it did not hurt), she was always relieved when he asked her to wait there; *it was better than being beaten.*

The *brown toilet* was Kebi's least favourite bathroom in the house. Aside from the fact that everything in it (toilet, sink, shower and floor) was dark brown, it only had one tiny window located above the toilet, which did not let in much air or light thus rendering the bathroom dark, humid and stuffy most of the time. More so, because it was centrally located in comparison to the other bathrooms in the house, it was the most easily accessible and was therefore overused and not cleaned as much as it was used. When George told her to wait for him there that afternoon, the floor was wet as usual and smelled of urine. When she got there, she managed to push herself up onto her feet and in doing so, felt a throbbing pain in her face. She was not tall enough to look into the mirror above the sink so she quickly grabbed a steel bucket, placed it upside-down and stood on top of it. When she saw her reflection in the mirror, she realised that ever since she had first started getting beaten months earlier, this was the first time she had ever looked at herself in a mirror. Although the left side of her face stung from where he hit her, it looked normal. On the other hand, her eyes were red and puffy from crying but when she looked more closely, she noticed a deep sadness in her eyes and instantly felt sorry for the little girl she was looking at.

God, please help me, she whimpered.

Tears streamed down her face as she continued to stare at her reflection then she heard him shout.

"You better be ready before I come there!"

She jumped off the bucket and undressed quickly despite her agonizing soreness then stood facing the door awaiting his arrival. He pushed the door open and with rage in his eyes he motioned for her to lie down. She obeyed without hesitation and lay on her stomach, as usual.

"Lie on your back!" he ordered.

Kebi thought it was odd for him to ask her to lie on her back but she quickly turned over. He dumped his weight on her and as though determined to teach her a lesson, he raped her vaginally for the very first time as she screamed.

Psychotherapy Session

STILL ON THE 18 BUS, Kebi was a bit anxious since it was now three fifty-three and the bus was moving at a snail's pace. As she considered getting off and making a run for it, she remembered she had not yet come up with a response if the therapist asked 'what brings you here today'. Her heart raced at the thought of this because she did not like being unprepared. She had wracked her brain for days trying to come up with a sensible response so she would not look stupid. The fact was, at work a couple of weeks earlier she had been involved in an incident which had continued to weigh on her mind. She expressed her concerns about the incident to a close colleague who suggested she seek therapy but she initially laughed off the idea.

"Dude, I don't do therapy; it's not for people like me," she said.

Her colleague was intrigued.

"What do you mean by it's not for people like you; therapy is for everyone."

She then retracted.

"I know it's for *everyone* but when it comes down to it, it just seems like a First World thing; I don't know anyone like me who has ever gone to therapy. Where I was raised, if you have a problem, you deal with it on your own. You don't go looking for some random person to talk to about personal problems."

Her colleague smiled.

"Trust me, it will help you in *so* many ways; I know people whose lives were completely transformed after they went to therapy."

She paused.

"I don't deny that it will help but there is a part of me that feels as though going to therapy is an admission of my inability to deal with normal issues which I am *supposed* to be able to deal with... do you get what I mean? It makes me feel like a weak person, which I am not."

"I understand what you mean but I don't agree," he said, "Acknowledging that there is a problem takes a lot of strength. Deciding to get professional help for it

10

takes even more strength. It is definitely not a display of weakness."

He went on to school her on the potential benefits of therapy and this made her realise that the negative impression she had of therapy was associated with a lack of knowledge about what it truly entailed. She decided to give it a try. With the help of her boss, her first therapy session was rapidly booked but with every passing day, she grew more anxious since she knew issues from her abusive childhood would likely come up. She was scared to reopen that abominable closet. She looked up the therapist online to find out what he might be like; he appeared warm and approachable in his LinkedIn profile, was also vastly experienced and worked for several reputable hospitals. She was certain she had nothing to worry about in that regard but was still increasingly nervous as she made her way there by bus that afternoon.

She heard the automated bus announcement: '*Next stop – Canal Bank.*' It was three-fifty-eight. She pressed the bell and made her way towards the door and no sooner did she get to it, did it swing open. Cheerily, she thanked the bus driver, dashed out onto the busy pavement and immediately spotted the therapist's office building. She ran towards it thinking, *what idiot goes to therapy not knowing what help they want?* As she neared the entrance of the building, she felt as though she was making a huge mistake. She took out her phone and scrolled down to the therapist's last email correspondence and was about to start typing an apology for not being able to make it to the session when someone stepped out of the building and held the door open for her, smiling. She thanked him and went in reluctantly as the door swung shut behind her. Then she saw his name 'EDWARD SWELLING', boldly imprinted on the wall to her left. She knocked on the door and went in.

As she sat waiting to be called, Kebi took several deep breaths. The receptionist had said *Edward would be out any minute* and Kebi's brain instantly went into over drive - *I really should have thought this through; an entire hour for one session; I have nothing worth talking about for even thirty minutes; I should probably just walk out now...*

She let out a loud sigh prompting the receptionist to turn to her, sweetly.

"You okay?"

Kebi nodded and smiled... *shit, now I can't leave.*

A deep male voice suddenly came through the door.

"Kebi?"

She was so startled she dropped her handbag on the floor.

"Yes... Here!"

She managed a smile as she sprang down on all fours, fumbling to pick up the contents of her handbag that were splattered all over the floor.

"Oh, I am so sorry," he said.

"It's okay... it's my fault, I wasn't paying attention," she said with a smile.

She quickly tossed everything into her bag.

"Hi, I am Kebi, nice to meet you."

He was bald and unexpectedly short with a warm smile as he held out his hand.

"Edward Swelling. It's a pleasure to meet you. My apologies for shouting out your name like that."

Kebi chuckled.

"It's okay, I was miles away."

He led her through to his office as he continued to offer apologies for having kept her waiting. She checked the time.

13

"It's okay; it looks like I was only out there for a couple of minutes."

They entered his office which was painted off-white, smelled like coffee and was sparsely furnished. A lone-curtained open window on the far side let in a cold breeze which prompted Edward to go over and close it *to keep out the noise,* he said. He gestured for Kebi to have a seat on a cosy crimson couch to the left of the room, next to which there was a side table with an opened box of tissues (just like she had seen in movies). She smiled because she appreciated his thoughtfulness in placing the box of tissues there although she knew she would not need them since hers was not the kind of problem to make one cry. Moreover, because she did not even want to be there, she knew she would be too self-conscious to cry. And finally, she never cried in public.

He cleared his throat as he sat down.

"Thank you for coming in."

"Of course, thank *you* for having me and for scheduling a meeting at such short notice."

Although she was not saying anything remotely important, she noticed he was *really* attentive while she spoke and that put her a little more at ease.

He said, "I felt the need to fit you in as quickly as possible mainly because your issue seemed quite urgent."

She immediately felt guilty that he had possibly put other appointments on hold in order to see her. Worse still, she had no clue how to let him know she did not intend to stay for the full hour of the session; speaking her mind had never been her forte. Trying not to come across as unappreciative, she attempted to give it a go.

"I am really extremely thankful to you for fitting me in so quickly... and I feel really bad but I kind of don't think I need therapy anymore... I don't really have any major issues that need fixing so I wasn't sure if I could maybe... cancel part of the session?"

Her mouth became dry and her heart raced because Edward's face was expressionless while she spoke. Then he nodded.

"Sorry, before we proceed, is it okay to refer to you as Kebi or by a different name... there's a second name on your notes..."

A bit surprised that he did not acknowledge a word of her train wreck of a speech, she replied.

"No, Kebi is fine."

He scribbled something quickly.

"Okay, I just have to let you know you have been offered twelve therapy sessions as per the agreement between me and your employer. As we go along, if you feel the need for fewer or more sessions, we can discuss that and make necessary adjustments."

What a relief, she thought.

Edward went on.

"Have you ever been to therapy?"

She was glad he asked because she had begun to feel like a fish out of water.

"No, this is my first time," she smiled.

"In therapy, all we aim to do is to work through the client's everyday challenges; that's really all it is."

She expected him to say more but that was it.

"Okay," she said.

He continued.

"How it works is, just like we arranged to meet today, we will schedule weekly sessions and if either of us needs to cancel a session, we would contact the other by email or you could give me a call... you have my office number, don't you?"

"Is it the one that's at the end of your emails?"

"That's the one. I'll also give you my card at the end of the session, just in case."

"Okay."

Edward cleared his throat.

"Earlier you said you did not think you needed therapy anymore..."

This time Kebi wanted to make sure she said the right thing without waffling along in an endless sentence.

"Erm... it's not that I don't think I need therapy, I just feel that maybe one therapy session might be enough because all I really need is some clarity on why I overreacted in the way I did during an incident at work recently."

Edward immediately referred to the sheet he was holding.

"I did receive brief notes from your boss about the incident... would *you* like to tell me what happened?"

She was ready to get it over with.

"Yes... I guess you have already gathered from my boss that I work at the sexual health clinic up the road..."

He looked at the sheet again.

"The Belvedere Clinic?"

"Yes... so, a couple of weeks ago I attended to a patient who basically left me rattled."

Edward seemed to wonder about something so Kebi stopped and pursed her lips to let him speak.

"Sorry to interrupt... what kind of work do you do at the clinic?"

"Sorry, I should have said so earlier... I do consultations with asymptomatic patients and also assist doctors in carrying out patient examinations."

He nodded.

"Right; do you ever attend to patients on your own or is it always with a doctor?"

"Yes, I work on my own when I attend to asymptomatic patients and also when collecting their samples."

"Okay. I was just trying to get a clear picture of how you worked."

"That's okay."

"Please continue, whenever you're ready."

Kebi regrouped, took a deep breath and continued.

"I attended to a patient in his late-fifties who lived in the Philippines but was visiting the UK two weeks ago. He came to our clinic for a routine sexual health screen and was first attended to by a health adviser who later handed him over to me to collect his samples for testing. The health adviser briefed me on the patient beforehand and stated that his preferred sex partners were teenage boys within the age of consent and that all additional information about the patient was in the database. I checked it out and casually proceeded to going out to get the patient from the waiting room. As he made his way towards me after I had called out his name, I felt a sudden rush of unexplained anxiety which I had never felt before. But I maintained my composure and warmly introduced myself then dutifully asked him to confirm his date of birth as we went towards the examination room. Once we got there, he spoke playfully.

'I don't know if you noticed my date of birth; I am very old... I'm nearly sixty!'

'Oh! The big 6-0!' I said pleasantly.

He continued to talk as I washed my hands.

'You, on the other hand... you look as young and as innocent as my little friends in the Philippines!'

I guessed he was referring to the teenage boys he had mentioned to my colleague.

'Your little friends?' I said.

He immediately seemed eager to talk about them as he nodded excitedly, sat down and carefully crossed one leg over the other.

'I am from England but I have lived in the Philippines for over six years now...' he said gleefully.

'Oh, okay. What's it like out there in the Philippines?'

With a look of excitement, he said, 'Oh it's marvellous! The food, the weather, the people...'

As I stood across from him putting on my gloves, he lowered his tone as if he was about to let me in on a secret.

'I was just telling your colleague earlier... I have a bunch of *gorgeous*-looking lads out there in the Philippines who I do consider as my best friends even though they are only in their teens.'

'Oh, how sweet, isn't it nice to have people you can call best friends...?' I said.

He was even more enthused as he went on.

'For sure, tell me about it darling... I'm so lucky to have them... you know, the thing is, as you can probably tell, I'm quite young at heart myself so I only surround myself with youngins.'

'With what?'

'Youngins.'

I had never heard that word before.

'Children,' he said.

'Oh okay.'

I smiled but suddenly felt another flush of anxiety. I did not feel like continuing to engage in the conversation about his teenage friends so as I sat down, I attempted to change the topic.

'Well, the blood tests we're going to do today are...'

He jumped in.

'So sorry to cut you off but you know what I said earlier about you looking like my little friends...'

'Mhm?'

I kept a straight face.

'It was *totally* meant as a compliment because you look so young and innocent.'

'Ah okay,' I said dismissively, 'so what I was trying to say about the blood tests was...'

'Sorry darling, sorry to cut in again, it's just I really think I might have offended you with what I said...'

Although he was absolutely right, I did not want to go into it because I was already uneasy and did not want to make it worse. I forced a smile.

'No, it is fine. I am not offended and thank you for the compliment.'

He seemed overly elated and threw his fist in the air.

'You're *more* than welcome, I am so glad you did not take it the wrong way... you know there are some people who are super sensitive to *everything* and even if you give them a compliment they take it really badly then you just don't know how to explain to them that it really was a compliment...'

He talked non-stop about his dislike for sensitive people and as he spoke, I wondered why I had thanked him for the 'compliment'. It bothered me that I had gone as far as saying 'thank you' for something which had in fact made me uneasy.

Then he said, 'Blimey, you're married, you can't be that young then!'

He seemed not to have any filter.

Mustering some courage, I said, 'Yes, I *am* married and if I'm honest, I find all this a bit inappropriate so...'

He placed his hand on my arm and exclaimed.

'Oh, I'm so sorry! I really am!'

Subtly, I moved my arm away from his touch.

'It's okay,' I said, 'let's just proceed with the tests otherwise we'll be here all day.'

I explained what the blood tests were for and proceeded to examine his arms for suitable veins. I noticed he was gazing at me but I decided not to pay it any mind. Once I began to take his blood samples, he started talking about his teenage friends again.

'...They're so polite and well-mannered and that's why I love them so much...'

I pretended to be engrossed in what I was doing since I did not want to engage in the conversation but that did not deter him from talking. A part of me felt bad about ignoring him because I was always friendly and pleasant to all my patients, no matter what.

He said, 'Sorry, did you say something?'

I had my eyes fixated on the syringe in his arm as I spoke.

'I didn't say anything but I'm listening. I'm just trying to finish taking these samples so you don't have to hang around here for too long.'

'Oh, thank you... has anyone ever told you you're really easy to talk to... you're such a good listener... you don't interrupt when...'

Without meaning to be overt, I sighed deeply.

He said, 'Oh, I'm sorry, I'm just going on and on. I hope that wasn't too personal...'

He was about to place his hand on my arm again but I raised it before he could touch it. I pretended to adjust my seat and continued to take his blood samples.

I said, 'No, it wasn't too personal. It's just I really need you to remain still so I can fill up the tubes a little faster.'

'Oh, sorry, I'm so sorry. Sometimes I'm worse than a teenager,' he chuckled.

He was quiet for a few seconds and I hoped he would remain like that until I finished taking all the samples.

'Now, with your arm still, it is flowing a lot faster,' I said.

He laughed.

'It's because I was acting like a child and got told off. From now on, I'll do whatever you say... anything at all... you know, the lads back home... they're *so* obedient.'

I said nothing. He paused then suddenly became serious.

'Everyone wonders why I prefer the lads out there and I know it's not fair to make general statements about people but those lads are super cool and easy.'

Once again, I felt a rush of anxiety and my heart began to race. I was uncomfortable with him saying the boys were easy but I smiled to conceal my discomfort.

'I see you smiling,' he said slyly, 'I know you know exactly what I mean.' He winked.

Once again, he lowered his tone as if he did not want anyone passing by to hear.

'These lads, I tell you, they will do *anything* you ask of them, anything whatsoever.'

I still said nothing and to my surprise, he too remained silent. The last tube was nearly full when I felt his gaze linger on my face for a little longer than I was comfortable with. It seemed he wanted to say something.

'All done,' I said.

'Thanks darling, erm, I'm not asking your age or anything but I would bet any money that you're not yet twenty-one.'

I felt uneasy around him and had had enough of his commentary so in that exact moment, I decided I would get someone else to collect the rest of his samples.

I took a deep breath and spoke as calmly as I could.

'I'm very sorry but I will get a colleague to come in and take over from me because I just remembered I've got to be somewhere else.'

He looked confused.

'But I thought *you* were going to take all the samples.'

'I was going to but just remembered I have to be somewhere else. I am really sorry about that, I have taken all the blood samples so my colleague will come in and collect the throat sample then they will explain to you how to obtain the rectal sample and where to leave it down the hall.'

'But why don't *you* take the bum sample while you're here?'

I shook my head.

'I'm very sorry but my colleague will explain to you how to do it, don't worry.'

Feigning urgency, I dashed to the sink and washed my hands as he continued to express his confusion about the situation. I did not realise he had come up next to me until he touched my upper arm.

'Did I say something to offend you, darling?' he said.

I was startled and instantly moved my arm away.

'Don't touch my arm,' I said sternly.

He seemed surprised at my tone.

'I'm so sorry, darling, I really am; I didn't mean to scare you.'

Without responding, I grabbed the blood samples and notes and headed for the door. The medical supplies' trolley was in the way so I stopped to push it out of my way.

He suddenly began to shout.

'This is ridiculous! Every time I attend this clinic my samples are taken by the same person! Why do I have to wait for someone else today?'

I could not believe he was raising his voice at me when *I* was the one who had endured his distasteful comments.

I said, 'First of all, can you please not shout. I told you I have to be somewhere else. Someone will come in immediately to collect the rest of the samples but if you keep up this behaviour, you will get kicked out.'

'Kicked out? Kicked out for what when you're standing here mouthing off instead of taking the fucking bum sample!'

Suddenly, he turned his back to me and pulled down his trousers; he bent over, pushed his butt cheeks apart and said, 'Take the fucking sample!'

I was stupefied and asked him to pull up his trousers but for some reason, I sounded like I was whispering. He mumbled something then when he turned to look at me, he quickly pulled up his trousers and began to apologise but I walked out. I stood outside the door for a couple of seconds because I did not quite know what to do. I felt so violated and noticed I was trembling. I had to hand him over to someone else to collect his remaining samples so I went to the laboratory across the hall and found a colleague who kindly took him over.

"Despite appearing calm outwardly, I was emotionally overwhelmed and hurried off to the staff room for a breather. Thankfully, it was empty when I got there so I remained there and wept. I was angry and blamed myself for all that happened."

"Why did you blame yourself?" Edward said.

She sighed.

"It was my fault; if I had firmly shut him down from the beginning, none of the other rubbish would have happened. I entertained his reckless comments and even thanked him for that stupid compliment; calling me darling and touching my arm... he actually touched my arm twice. Who does he think he is?"

She paused.

"The whole situation made me feel so stupid."

Edward observed her quietly and let her have a moment to herself.

He said, "What in particular would you say made you feel stupid?"

She sighed.

"Just the fact that I did not speak up... and when I did speak to him I was not assertive... I don't understand why. I do this every single time. I don't speak up."

Edward said, "Did you speak to anyone about the incident?"

"I kind of did but not fully... I spoke to the same colleague who encouraged me to come to therapy but I did not give him all the details of what happened between me and the patient."

Edward nodded, "Was there any reason why you omitted some details?"

She gave him a surprised look as though he *should* know what the reason was.

"I was embarrassed."

"What were you embarrassed about?"

"It was embarrassing to let anyone know that I could not stand up for myself. The mere fact that he pulled down his pants and demanded that I take his bum sample implies that there must have been something about me that made him have no respect for me. You don't meet someone for the first time and disrespect them in such an extreme manner unless you sense that you can. I completely let myself down... you have no idea."

Edward said, "I understand and I am sorry you went through that; there were obviously some boundaries that were crossed."

She shrugged, "I guess there *were* boundaries that were crossed but you know what... I'm okay now... I guess I was just surprised at my reaction and what I needed was clarity on why he affected me so profoundly... no one has ever had such an effect on me."

She paused to think about why it *had* affected her so much.

Edward said, "Why were you surprised at your reaction?"

Kebi chuckled.

"I was just wondering the same thing... I don't know."

"I mean, why were you surprised that you were affected so profoundly?"

"Oh I see what you mean; it's because I'm not easily moved by things."

"What do you mean?"

"It's hard to explain... I'm usually calm and controlled no matter what; even when I am in a stressful situation. So it was completely out of character for me to be mentally and visibly affected by a person like him."

Edward said, "What do you mean by *a person like him*?"

"I just mean a person like him who chooses to have sex with young boys and brags about how easy they are."

Edward nodded.

"You're saying you did not like him bragging about it."

"Yeah, I mean, I don't know for sure the ages of the boys but just knowing that they are teenagers was unsettling. Although I was informed that they were within the age of consent, honestly, it still made me uneasy."

"I understand..."

He turned to her notes.

"I am not sure if you would like to touch on this but it was mentioned in your notes that you were molested when you were a child?"

Kebi had been so engrossed in the discussion that it totally slipped her mind that there was a chance her abusive past would come up. Caught off guard, she tried to dismiss it.

"Yes, I was but I have healed from it; it doesn't really affect me anymore."

Edward remained silent and she felt compelled to fill the silence so she explained further.

"It used to affect me a lot but talking about it over the years has made it easier... now it doesn't even feel like it happened to me."

He leaned in slightly.

"I am sorry you went through that."

Kebi gave a nonchalant shrug.

"Thank you."

He continued, "Just going back to something you said earlier..."

"Okay..."

"You said the molestation during your childhood no longer affects you... did you get any sort of counselling for it?"

She shook her head

"No."

"So how were you able to heal from it?"

"I love to write so from a young age I wrote down my feelings which in essence, helped to get rid of the pain. And as an adult, I talk about it so I have always had an outlet and that has helped me heal."

Edward asked, "How long ago did it happen?"

"You mean my rape?"

"Yes."

"I was eight when it first started and it continued for nearly four years."

He looked surprised but did not say anything and once again, Kebi felt the need to explain.

"It happened in Cameroon, where I grew up. There were about thirty of us living in my dad's house and we also had a house girl who was paid to cook, clean and do laundry. Unfortunately, she didn't last very long with us because apparently she was sluggish and inefficient. As soon as she left, my mom insisted on replacing her with a house boy rather than another house girl. She said she wanted someone who was physically stronger and more able to perform household tasks as well as to keep the house secure. And in came George, a twenty-seven year old, to work as the house boy."

Once again, Kebi noticed how attentive Edward was and it put her even more at ease.

"When George first came to meet my parents, I remember being seated at the dining table with them and I noticed that as they spoke to him, he kept his hands clasped behind his back, looked downwards and said 'Yes, Sah' and 'Yes, Madam' excessively. At the time, I wondered why he never let them finish a sentence before saying 'Yes, Sah' or 'Yes, Madam' but I soon learned that it was his way of showing them how attentive and respectful he was. No sooner had he come to see my parents on that first day did he move in to start work. He was shown around briefly and was allocated a room at the boys' quarters and the next day, he woke up very early (even before my mom), and started to clean. He was strategic and very organized. Before we left for school, he cleaned the car so my uncle did not have to, he polished everyone's shoes before they remembered to, he did everyone's laundry although he was not asked to and he cleaned magnificently. He always seemed to be a step ahead especially in comparison to the former house girl and therefore quickly became the topic of conversation amongst my parents during our car rides to school – he was their dream come true."

"What was he like with you and your siblings?" Edward said.

"He made everything easier - he served us lunch at the dining table (that is, he literally placed our plates at the table so we did not have to), sat with us while we ate and never let us clear the table afterwards despite the fact that we told him we normally did all that ourselves. He even insisted on helping with homework although, straight out of the gate, it was clear that he did not read or write well. He grossly mispronounced words and whenever I corrected his pronunciations, he smiled eerily and repeated it in the same wrong way. At some point, I stopped correcting him because I had a feeling he did not like it."

"Sorry to cut in," Edward said, "We have five minutes left in the session."

"Oh, okay."

She could not believe an hour had gone by and regretted that the session was nearly over.

Grooming

EDWARD HAD SAID they would pick up from where they left off and although she wondered how he would remember where they stopped (since he did not take any notes), she felt a sense of eagerness as she headed out to her second session a week later. Always one to document her feelings, whilst on the bus, she took out her notebook and wrote:

I feel like I can tell Edward everything...

He'll be the first person I have ever told everything to...

When he greeted her, she felt a deeper level of familiarity with him than she did the last time.

"How have you been since the last session?" he said.

"I've been good - everything's been okay, thank you."

He smiled, "Good... so, last week while talking about your childhood, we stopped at the point where you decided to stop correcting the house boy's pronunciations because of his ominous reaction."

"Yes."

"Did the dynamic between you and him change at all after that?"

"Yes it changed drastically."

"Would you like to elaborate on how it changed?"

"Sure. It changed over time but the first time I ever realised he was not as nice as he made out was when he reprimanded me for going out one day. My dad never allowed us to visit our friends but we still went out to play with them when he was at work. My mom was more lenient and even allowed us to go on play dates. One day, she said I could go and play at my neighbour's house. When I returned, George pulled me by the arm and asked where I had been. I told him my mom had given me permission to go out and he whispered sternly in my ear, warning me never to leave the house again even if my mom said I could. He said my dad was the authority and that he would tell my dad that my mom had let me go out."

"Did you speak to your mom about this?"

"No, I did not want to cause trouble between my parents."

"How old were you then?"

"I was eight... this happened a few weeks after George moved in."

"As far as you can remember, did anyone else notice that side of him?"

"I don't think anyone noticed because they talked very highly of him. My dad gave him a lot of power too soon; he was in charge of looking after me and my brothers and was lauded for encouraging us to be more independent by getting us to do menial household chores. Personally, I did not mind doing them because before he moved in, I did them nearly every day. I was keen to show him how hardworking I was but unfortunately, he was critical of everything I did. The more he criticized me, the more chores I did. Ironically, he told my dad I was hard working and my dad encouraged me to keep it up."

Edward paused.

"What was your relationship like with your dad?"

"My dad was very complimentary, loving and generous; I thrived off his compliments. He always referred to me as beautiful but also described me as 'ambitious', 'eloquent' and 'self-disciplined', three words which I had not heard of before but because of how he said them, I believed they meant I was special in some way. He was extremely hard working and had been the breadwinner of his immediate and extended family throughout his life so he was very much in control of everyone and everything. He was widely respected and was also feared for his financial power but at home he was feared for his *modus operandi* which was: 'If you spare the rod, you spoil the child'. So... yeah...that helped to keep the house in order."

Edward needed clarification.

"So you got beaten by your dad as a form of discipline?"

"We did but I think it sounds worse than it really was; there were many of us in the household; children, teenagers and young adults and it helped my dad to keep everyone in check. But I think I was the only one who never got beaten by my dad."

"Why was that?"

41

"I don't think it was deliberate; it just happened to be the case."

"And how did that make you feel?"

She paused to think about it.

"I don't think I had any specific feelings about it; it actually only occurred to me that I had never been beaten by my dad when George started beating me."

Edward looked a little surprised.

"George, the house boy?"

"Yeah, he started beating me quite randomly actually; it started with the chores... I tried so hard to impress him but he always put me down. Somehow, before I knew it, I was doing nearly all the housework on my own; I mopped and swept, washed and ironed, and even dusted furniture that was three times my height. I did these after school and even when my grandmother lived with us, she never really noticed how much work I did. I disliked coming home from school because all I did was housework. George even stopped cooking for us and when we got home from school, he instructed me (at times, from the comfort of his bed) to cook our meals."

"You mentioned your grandmother lived with you?"

"She did sometimes; she lived several hours away in the village but visited us and stayed for months at a time."

"How did she not notice you doing all of George's housework?"

Kebi sighed.

"First of all, she was older so she moved around slowly and whenever she saw me doing house work, she was pleased and encouraged me to keep it up. She was none the wiser and sadly, the more I was praised the more obliged I felt to keep working although I was tired. This was actually what led to George hitting me the very first time. After school one day, I dozed off while doing laundry in the backyard. He found me asleep and slapped me across the face saying he would tell my dad about it and that my dad would be disappointed in me."

"Did he tell your dad?"

"No."

"Did *you* tell your dad?"

Kebi looked surprised.

"I thought I was wrong to have fallen asleep while doing laundry so there was no way I was going to report myself to my dad. At the time, I believed George was justified in hitting me."

Edward paused.

"Had he hit you before that?"

"That was the first time he hit me."

"I'm sorry you had to go through that."

Kebi chuckled.

"That was nothing compared to what he did next."

Edward looked on as she proceeded.

"From that point on, things changed for the worst quite rapidly; I began to see his evil side more frequently. One afternoon, he came and sat with us while we did our homework at the front porch, then we heard my mom's car pull up outside. He suddenly dashed into the house and returned with a Bible and sat next to me. As my mom walked in, he began to read the Bible out aloud and she seemed impressed and praised him for teaching me Bible stories. I vividly remember this particular incident because I believed it was the first time I had experienced his duplicity."

"Did you ever consider talking to your parents about this?"

Kebi nodded continuously.

"I did... I always did but was too scared to say anything."

"What were you scared of?"

Kebi had never thought about this before; she reflected for a moment.

"I was scared of George... it's hard to explain. I must have been brainwashed or something. He knew I was close with my dad and no sooner had he moved in, did he begin to plant seeds of doubt in my head (towards my dad). He told me my dad did not really think I was smart; he said adults lied to children all the time so as not to hurt their feelings with the truth. For some reason, I believed him but of course now I know that his goal was to have sex with me. If a paedophile is around a child and has sexual urges towards that child, they will do whatever they need to do to have sex with them. In my case, it was important for him to distance me from everyone (especially my parents). What facilitated this was the fact that I spent more time with him than I did with my dad or any other adult and he talked to me a lot about how pretentious adults really were; so I progressively viewed my parents as untrustworthy. It was all part of the grooming process."

"Was there anyone else you could have spoken to?"

Kebi reflected again.

"I'm trying to think back... there were lots of adults in the house but not once did I even consider speaking to any of them... I am not sure why... I just remember feeling unable to trust anyone."

"That sounds like a not-so-nice position to be in at eight years old."

"Yeah, it was hard but soon after the incident with the Bible I stupidly decided to stand up to him on my own. One day, I told him I had noticed he no longer did much work; he lashed out and told me to keep my *big mouth shut* otherwise he would tell my dad about all the times when I had been naughty. Unfortunately, from then on he never let anyone see me do certain chores anymore. He locked me in my parents' bathroom where I did mounds of laundry and ironing after school. Consequently, I spent less time with Ebot and Junior in the afternoons since I was locked away in the bathroom."

"How did you feel about not spending time with your brothers after school?" Edward asked.

She sighed as memories from her childhood raced through her mind.

"It was horrible. We used to laugh so much together then we became so quiet. My brothers never smiled anymore... they always looked sad... they didn't deserve that."

"None of you deserved it... you were just kids."

Kebi could not hold back her tears.

"We did everything he asked us to do and if we didn't do it to his satisfaction, he scolded us more viciously. I was scared to say a word and told my brothers not to, either. And just like that, we began to live in fear in our own home."

First Exposure

KEBI HAD BEEN LOOKING FORWARD to her third therapy session. Following her second, she started experiencing a recurrence of vivid dreams like she had during her childhood and teenage years.

She said to Edward, "Not only have I become more emotional in the past week but there has been a surge in the frequency of my nightmares. I keep having the same dreams night after night just like I did throughout my teenage years and this has begun to take a toll on me."

Edward knew this was expected.

"Given how much you have delved into your past in recent weeks, it is not surprising that you are more emotional. It is part of the healing process but we can work on finding ways to deal with the emotional stress it is putting on you."

She looked emotionally drained as she stared emptily at Edward.

"I sometimes wish I had amnesia so I would forget everything that happened. These memories disappeared for many years and now they're back with a vengeance; everywhere I turn, there seems to be a reminder of something from the past; I am not even able to be fully present with my kids without a torturous memory popping into my head. I just want to be normal but the reminders are getting in the way of my life."

Edward remained silent as she went on.

"Last night, I relived an incident which I had long forgotten."

She paused then continued.

"One evening, when my relatives and I were hanging out in our front yard, George asked me to come in and show him where I had kept *the envelope*. I did not know what envelope he was referring to but followed him into the kitchen where he asked me to wash the pots and pans that were in the sink. I was not surprised he lied about an envelope to get me to wash the dishes but I was more intent on washing up quickly so I could go back outside. As soon as I started washing, he left the kitchen; I had been washing up for a few minutes when I heard someone walk in behind me. I turned and saw that it was him so I continued washing then he said my name. I turned around again and he had pulled down his trousers exposing his penis. I was shocked and stood still with my back to him. I was confused as to why he was showing me his penis but he pretended to be surprised at my reaction.

'Why are you not looking at it? Have you never seen your brother's own?'

Although he spoke in a low tone, I could tell he had moved closer to me. He touched my shoulder and I dropped the pot I was washing and ran to the bedroom I shared with Ebot and Junior. I shut the door behind me and sat at the edge of my bottom-bunk bed wondering what that was about. Moments later, he came in and stood in the doorway holding the door open and asked why I had run away. I didn't know what to say and could not even look at him since I was embarrassed to have seen his penis. He carefully pushed the door shut and came towards me. My heart raced as I looked downward to avoid looking at him.

He stood right in front of me and casually pulled out his penis again.

'Look at it,' he smiled.

I felt as if I could not breathe and started to cry. With his penis still exposed, he touched my left cheek and whispered, 'Why are you crying? I was just playing with you and now you are crying. Okay sorry, stop crying.'

He pulled up his trousers with a chuckle and explained he did not mean to make me cry and that he felt bad – he even asked if I had forgiven him and I said yes. He said not to tell my mom otherwise she might get upset with him since she would not understand that he was joking. He wiped my eyes then we both heard a door open in the corridor. He turned around promptly and left. That night, I pondered what had happened and for some reason, I believed I had overreacted by running away and crying."

Edward asked, "Did you tell anyone about this incident?"

Kebi shook her head; Edward handed her another box of tissues.

"Thank you," she sobbed, "It is not easy to understand what my mind set was at that time. I was gullible and naive and George knew I would never report him; that's why he continued. For many years... and even as an adult, I blamed myself for not speaking up."

Edward leaned toward her.

"It was not your fault."

Kebi took a deep breath and closed her eyes in an attempt to regain her composure. After a moment of silence, she remembered something she wanted to share with Edward.

"After exposing his penis to me, he became more audacious; I woke up early one morning and found that I had been assigned to clean the *brown toilet*. I cleaned it and had a quick shower there but just when I was drying myself off, the door swung open and in walked George (I had forgotten to lock the door). He looked at me, surprised, as he shut the door.

'Why are you covering your body with the towel?' he said.

'I am drying myself.'

'Continue bathing,' he said casually.

'I've finished.'

'Finished what?' he pointed at my soapy feet, 'Look at your legs.'

As I looked to see what he was referring to he scolded, 'Put it down and continue bathing.'

'But I've finished bathing, Uncle George,'

He charged towards me saying, 'I will drag you on the floor with this towel if you don't put it down now!'

He grabbed it from me and I immediately rinsed the soap off my legs while he watched.

When I had finished he scolded me.

'Turn this way and wash them properly.'

He wanted me to turn and face him but for some reason, I instead gathered water in my cupped hands and poured it onto my feet without turning to face him. I turned off the tap and extended my left hand so he would hand me the towel but he did not.

'I've finished rinsing them,' I said again.

'Turn so I can see.'

"I turned around and faced him…"

Kebi suddenly paused and Edward noticed she was fighting back tears.

She spoke slowly.

"At the time, I still showered with Ebot and Junior nearly every day and was unaware of the importance of not letting others see us naked. Despite this, I will never forget how uneasy I felt as George gazed at my naked eight year old body without saying a word. After a little while of him staring, I heard my mom call out to him; he instantly tossed the towel to me and left. I stood there and sobbed quietly."

After another long pause, Kebi smiled.

"Even as I cried, I tried to make sense of why I was crying and I could not. In my mind, he had not done or said anything hurtful so I could not understand why I felt uneasy when all he did was look at me."

Edward sighed.

"Please take a moment if you need to, there is no rush."

She sighed.

"I have never spoken about this and many other things that happened during my childhood because they are too painful to think about; but now I feel strong enough to walk through the pain so I am bent on getting everything out."

Edward nodded.

"I understand."

"Later that day, George asked if I knew what *Faytex* was?'

Edward looked puzzled.

"*Faytex* is a brand of sanitary pads used in Cameroon."

"Oh..." Edward nodded.

"I told George I knew what it was and he asked how I knew; I said I had seen my mom use it. He then went on to ask me a slew of questions regarding how and why she used sanitary pads; I did not know much and he mockingly said he would teach me about menses but that I would have to keep it a secret. In the same conversation, he asked if I knew what kissing was and I said no but the look on his face told me he knew I was lying. All I knew was, whenever people kissed on television, my dad instructed us to go to our room immediately. That was why I did not want George to find out that I knew what kissing was since I felt it was bad."

Kebi began to cough.

"Would you like some water?" Edward asked.

She smiled in appreciation.

"No, thank you, I was just clearing my throat."

"Sorry, you were saying you did not want George to find out you knew what kissing was."

"Yes but that conversation with him ignited something in me that made me want to tell my mom what he had been saying to me. However, I feared that because she liked him a lot, she would just give him a pat on the wrist. Despite all this, I still decided to take the risk and tell my mom. Later that day, I went to her room and sat at the tail end of her bed as she lay reading an issue of *Woman's Own* magazine. I greeted her and she asked how I was then continued to read while I sat quietly, trying to figure out what to say and what not to mention. I knew if I told her I had been doing all of George's chores, she would be upset that I had not told her sooner. But there were other things she did not know about; like him coming into the bathroom while I showered, asking about sanitary pads and about kissing. I decided to start off with the topic of sanitary pads which I felt she would be the least upset about."

'Mama...'

'Mhm,' she didn't take her eyes off the magazine.

'This morning Uncle George asked if I knew what pads were.'

She looked a bit surprised but kept her eyes on what she was reading.

'Why did he ask you?' she said.

I shrugged my shoulders as I became a little worried since her temperament had changed.

'I don't know... he asked if I knew what they were used for.'

She finally looked at me.

'And what did you say?'

This was *not* the reaction I was expecting; it sounded like I was already in trouble. Would she be mad that I told George I had seen her put pads in her underwear?

'Erm, I didn't say anything.'

She kept her gaze on me and I could tell she knew I was lying. She was quiet for a moment then turned back to her magazine.

'They better not bring those their dirty habits here,' she said.

I did not know what dirty habits she was referring to but I was relieved not to have told her what I actually told George about seeing her use pads in her underwear. She turned a page over and continued reading. I felt brave enough to bring up the next topic.

'Uncle George also asked if I knew something called menses.'

Again, she kept her eyes on the magazine in front of her.

'And what did you say?'

'I told him I don't know what it is... because I've never heard of it before.'

Although I was not facing her at this point, I guessed her silence meant she was thinking about what I had just told her. But she said nothing more and for some reason, I too said nothing further. After a while, I went to my room and lay in bed wondering if she was upset with me. That evening, George called me to the backyard and grabbed me by the ear.

'You went and told Mama that I asked you about *Faytex*!'

My ear stung as I desperately tried to release myself from his grip.

'Sorry, Uncle George, I didn't mean to report you.'

'Shut up!'

His fist landed on my jaw. I was shocked; it felt as though my jaw had been ripped out of my face and I screamed and doubled over clutching my face. Instantaneously, he seemed remorseful.

'Look at what you have caused; wait let me see.'

He put his palm over my cheek and rubbed it gently.

'Ah, Kebi sorry, don't cry again. Wait here; let me get something to press it with.'

He dashed into the house and got a wet cloth with which he massaged my face.

'You have to be careful with these things; you should not tell Mama everything me and you discuss. Look at what you have done. Do you think Mama will be happy if she sees your face like this? We have to make sure she does not see it; let me press it again.'

He massaged my face for a while longer and asked me to go in and look at it in a mirror to see if it looked okay. I did and came back to him.

'It looks okay; I can't see anything.'

He re-wet the cloth and asked me to hold it against my face for a little longer as he tearfully explained that he was the sole breadwinner for his impoverished

59

family and that my parents had saved his life by giving him a job. I felt bad for him and I kept my mouth shut.

A few days later, my dad summoned everyone for a family meeting before the older kids set off for the school term at boarding school. At the meeting, he praised George for always treating *the younger children* (me, Ebot and Junior) as his brothers and sisters and he encouraged him to keep it up.

When the school term began, George became completely different; he told my dad lies to make me appear recalcitrant and this resulted in my dad scolding me nearly every day. One day after school, George found out that I had scored nine out of ten in a maths test; he asked why I did not get all the questions right and I was casually explaining that I had misunderstood the question, when he suddenly slapped me and asked me to be quiet.

I was stunned and started crying but he shouted all the more.

'Wipe those crocodile tears! If Papa sees this test paper, he will break your back!'

I was confused because I had performed well in the test. *Did he not understand that scoring nine out of ten was good?*

He went on.

'Stop looking at me as if I don't have sense! Go and bring a cane, Papa will deal with you today!'

I did not quite understand what he meant but because I knew that his level of literacy was not up to par, I usually went along with whatever he said instead of correcting him. On this occasion, I was not worried because he clearly misunderstood the implication of my test score; my dad had never beaten me before and certainly was not going to beat me because of it; but I went to get a cane anyway since George seemed keen to get one ready for my dad to use on me later. I cut a long branch from our hibiscus flower hedge and handed it to him. In one motion, he snatched it and whipped my arm shouting.

'Is this a cane?'

I was stunned; I had never been whipped with anything before. It was strange. He carried on whipping me all over my body, saying *is this a cane* with every stroke. I screamed and ran toward the back of the house where my grandmother was having a nap. George ran after me and threatened to beat me for longer if I did not return to the front yard immediately. It was term-time so there was no one else at home but us (and my grandmother).

I returned to the front yard with him and he gave me ten additional strokes on my palms after which he ordered me to kneel down and listen closely.

'Papa said I should beat you if you fail in school. If you don't want me to beat you again, make sure you pass your tests.'

I was still sobbing from the throbbing pains in my hands.

'But I only failed one question,' I implored.

'But I only failed one question,' he mimicked, 'Look at your big mouth... ugly face... did you not hear what Papa said in the meeting?'

I shook my head as I had no clue what he was referring to.

'You better stop shaking that big head!' He whipped me again and lifted a finger to his lips as I screamed.

He said, 'Were you not there when Papa said I should take you as my brothers and sisters?'

I nodded.

'Ehein! As my brothers and sisters, if you fail your test, I will discipline you like Papa.'

"Did he ever beat your brothers?"Edward asked.

"Yes."

Edward looked surprised as Kebi explained.

"I vividly remember the first time he beat my six year old brother, Ebot. We had returned from school and our uniforms were dirty but Ebot's shirt also had dark brown marks that looked like chocolate stains. George asked him to kneel down and explain where the brown marks had come from. The more he said he did not know, the more George whipped him (on his palms) with the buckled end of my dad's belt. I had never seen anything like that before. It left me traumatised especially because Ebot was so little. After the beating, we went to our bedroom where I got a chance to massage his hands and I found myself crying because they looked very sore. George suddenly appeared in the doorway and said it seemed I was trying to win a crying competition and he ordered me to cry non-stop for half an hour and said if I stopped he would whip me. For the next half hour, he laughed while I cried and he still whipped me. I looked around at some point and Ebot had disappeared. That made me smile."

Victim or Culprit

SINCE STARTING THERAPY, Kebi struggled to be fully present with her children. This heightened her determination to address her childhood abuse issues and thereby resulted in an exponential increase in the documentation of her thoughts and feelings. When Edward greeted her on the afternoon of her fourth session, he recapped what they had covered in previous sessions and asked if there was anything else she specifically wanted to talk about.

"I wouldn't say there was anything new that I feel the need to talk about. However, this past week has been difficult; the nightmares have not stopped and there has been a sudden outpouring of horrific memories which basically haunt me day and night. I have had memories of random things like me and my brothers being beaten for eating too slowly, vomiting our food because we were forced to eat too quickly, beaten for coming in through the gate too slowly after school, for taking too long in the toilet, for not being able to give a reasonable explanation for why we were smiling at each other..."

Edward listened quietly as Kebi's eyes welled up with tears. She went on.

"He walked around with a stick in hand waiting for us to misstep so he would whip us. He also beat us with cables, shoes, brooms and even once threw stones at me. Since we were not allowed to cry during beatings, Ebot and I learned not to cry; then he said because we no longer cried it meant the canes he used were not effective. From then on, he mostly used a heavy wooden pestle (that was normally used to pound *fufu*) to beat us and evidently, we developed more fractures."

"Did your parents notice your injuries?"

"They did. We went to the hospital regularly to have X-rays and treatment but George made up lies which we told my parents about how we sustained the injuries; we usually said we fell off the swing or monkey bar in school.'

Edward shook his head in disbelief as he listened on.

66

"Thankfully, for some reason George reduced the frequency of Ebot's beatings but unfortunately, he decided to beat *me* in his place whenever he was 'disobedient'. The increase in my beatings rendered me sore a lot of the time and it had a huge impact on my ability to focus in class. My academic performance dropped drastically and this caught my dad's attention. One day, he called me into his room to find out what was going on. I said nothing."

Edward said, "Why did you not tell your dad about what was going on?"

Kebi sighed as she thought about it.

"I remember *exactly* how I felt when he asked me; I did not think he cared about me so I did not care to say anything."

She paused.

"George was extremely manipulative and he used even the most insignificant instances to demonstrate why I should not trust my dad. Someone once came over to visit my dad but he did not want to see them so he told George to say he was not home. George immediately pointed that out to me so I could see firsthand, what he had been telling me about not trusting my dad. Although he managed to distance me from my dad, I did not feel particularly distanced from my mom but I worried about what would happen this time if I told her about the beatings. I was in constant pain and it was at times unbearable and that was the main reason why I wanted to tell her about it. I wrote out what I would say to her and practised how I would say it without crying, for I did not want her to feel sad or guilty. I read it over and over so I would remember what to say and just like before, I went in one afternoon and sat on her bed while she was reading a magazine. But out of nowhere, I burst into tears. She got up and asked what was going on but I was so nervous that I struggled to get my words out. She placed a hand on my back and gently asked me to calm down. *She* seemed calm; she always appeared calm no matter what. As I tried to stop crying, I suddenly started gasping for air and it felt like I was suffocating.

I took some deep breaths and blurted out, 'Mama, it's Uncle George who has been beating us.'

I had never seen her so shocked in my life.

'What!'

She screamed so loud, a shiver ran down my spine.

I don't think I said much more after that because it turned into sheer chaos as she cried and screamed hysterically. That was the first time I had ever seen her cry and I felt a tremendous amount of guilt knowing I had caused it. She sounded so desolate.

She wailed, 'You read about these things in newspapers and don't know that they are happening in your own house, to your own children!'

She stormed out shouting.

'Where is he?'

Although I was anxious about what would happen, I followed slowly behind as relatives gathered around asking what had happened. My mom was screaming and threatening to kill George when my grand aunt asked someone to go and find him; he had gone to a nearby convenience store. As we awaited his return, I was grilled ferociously about why I had not told anyone about the beatings; I was blamed and shouted at and some even said it served me right for keeping it quiet.

He returned soon after and the household went into a frenzy of rage as he was confronted in the yard. His presence alone made me quiver and when he shouted and denied everything, I was so scared that I retreated into the main house and listened to the chaos from the kitchen window. He shouted and swore on his parents' lives that he had only ever beaten me once. He even went as far as asking how come no one had ever heard us cry if he truly beat us regularly. He sounded so convincing that even *I* wondered if it had simply been a bad dream. To my surprise, the clamour died down quickly and they sat around and listened to him talk then my grandmother called out to me.

'Where is Kebi? Tell her to come and face him and say what happened.'

I was terrified to come face-to-face with him but slowly made my way out. As soon as he saw me, he burst into tears dramatically.

'Kebi, why are you doing this?'

'I am not doing anything,' I said nervously.

He cut me off and called me a liar and a spoilt child and my grandmother scolded him.

'Shut your mouth, you foolish boy! Do you not have any respect for your elders sitting right here in front of you?'

He apologized and she proceeded to rebuking him vehemently for beating me up; she said whether he had beaten me one time or a thousand times was not the point; it should never have happened and he was wrong. She continued to reprimand him for what seemed like a really long time while my mom sat quietly next to her. Moments later, my dad drove in; the look on his face told me he was aware of what had happened. He forced a smile at me as he walked past and when he disappeared into the house, my grandmother addressed me in our tribal dialect (which George did not understand).

She said, 'Kebi, before we take this problem to your father, I will ask you one last time: This young man here says he only ever beat you once... is he telling the truth?'

I responded in our dialect saying he was lying. It was disheartening that she needed me to reconfirm what I had already told them – but it proved that George was right all along; for months, he had said no one would believe me if I told them he beat me. My grandmother and a couple of older relatives threw question after question at me and as I answered, it felt as though I was on trial. It hurt my feelings.

"What did they ask you?" Edward said.

"They asked to know where everyone was when George beat us... what he beat us with... why no one ever heard us cry... why we did not have scars... why I had not told anyone... was I sure about what I was saying... they even threatened to punish me if they found out I was lying. It was hurtful that they doubted me but I knew it was because they had never seen the evil side of George. All they knew about him was what he had chosen to present to them. When the interrogation was over, my grand aunt, who was the eldest in the household, reiterated (to him) that he was wrong to have taken the law into his hands and she hoped it would not happen again – she praised him for his hard work and dedication. He in turn, apologised endlessly and mumbled something inaudible to which my grand aunt said he need not worry, for she would ensure that my dad did not fire him. My heart dropped when I heard that. I hoped that the look on my dad's face earlier was a reflection of how angry he was and that George would get sent away based on that.

My grand aunt, grandmother and an older uncle continued to rain advice on George and after a while I realised other conversations around us were relatively subdued. I overheard someone say George was too calm and did not seem like the kind to beat children, another suggested that he might have had a difficult day and lost his temper, a couple of others concluded that as I was getting older, as expected, I had begun to tell lies, and an aunt even concluded that I must have lied about it happening more than once because I had never been beaten by anyone before. I was deeply hurt by their comments and pretended not to eavesdrop but I was more mortified when I looked up and realised my mom and George were nowhere in sight. I panicked as I looked around wondering where they were and moments later, we were summoned to the living room for a family meeting with my dad. When I got there, George was on his knees facing my parents, who were seated solemnly.

When everyone was seated, my dad said he had spoken to George and my mom privately and heard their versions of what had happened and that he wanted to ask George once again before everyone present.

He said, 'George, have you been beating the children mercilessly, to the point of breaking their bones?'

George flung his arms in the air and shook his head as he shouted.

'Papa, I beat them only one time, Sah, only one time.'

My dad turned to me smiling oddly.

'Kebi, is this true?'

'No, Papa it is not true, he...'

'Kebi, why?' George cut me off, 'What did I do to you?'

'Let her speak,' my dad said, 'Kebi, how many times did he beat you?'

He seemed keen to hear me out unlike everyone who had cross-examined me earlier.

'Many times,' I replied softly.

'How many times is many times?'

'I can't say the exact number but it was many times...'

'I said how many times!' he shouted, 'Kebi, have you started telling lies?'

I was stunned - he sounded like he did not believe me.

'I am not lying Papa; he beat us nearly every day...'

George jumped in and began to rant.

'I told you to do your homework. Instead, you went to play.'

'Papa, he is lying!'

'I beat you one time and now you say I beat you many times.'

'He is lying, Papa!'

George turned and addressed everyone present.

'When I beat her that one time, she said I have no right to beat her because her father has never beaten her. Papa, I am very sorry for beating your daughter. I wanted her read her book. You are very good to me and I will never disrespect you. You have helped me and my poor family in the village, I am very sorry, Sah...'

I could not believe all he was saying.

'He is lying, Papa! It is not true!'

My dad seemed furious.

'What is not true?'

'Everything he is saying is not true.' I said tearfully.

My dad got up and stepped towards me.

'I said, what is not true, Kebi? That you play too much? That your grades have dropped drastically? That you think we pluck money from trees to send you to school? And that when this young man who I pay to take care of you tries to correct you, you say he mistreats you?'

I sobbed helplessly, 'No, Papa...'

'Shut up, my friend!'

I was extremely hurt that he did not believe me and I looked in my mom's direction for help but she stared at me blankly as my dad spoke to George again.

'How many times did you beat her?'

George stuck with his story and continued to apologize.

'What did you beat her with?'

'A belt, Sah.'

'Which belt?'

'A belt from your room, Sah.'

He maintained a downward gaze and pretended to wipe a tear. I glanced over and when our eyes met he glared at me and I looked away. My dad continued.

'Is that what he used?'

'Yes, Papa, but he has used different things at other times...'

As I spoke, I noticed the disappointed look in my dad's face and I trailed off. We were both silent as he sat back down and continued to stare at me with regret. George grabbed the opportunity to continue pleading his case.

'I am sorry, Sah, I made a mistake. Even sometimes when it is time to eat, they instead go and play with their friends outside.'

He went on and on, and no one even tried to stop him which was surprising because during our family meetings, no one but my dad ever really spoke; and you only spoke if he spoke to you. George's endless rant was a reflection of how much power my dad had bestowed upon him.

'He's lying!' I pleaded again.

I looked at my mom again but she did not look my way - I desperately wanted her to say something because I knew she knew I was telling the truth. My grand aunt finally jumped in and told George to be quiet, stating that he had said enough.

She said, 'Kebi, wipe your eyes, please, don't cry, we don't like seeing you cry.'

She turned to my dad and spoke in our dialect.

'My son, please do not be angry with your daughter. She is just a child and children make mistakes. Sometimes children see things differently from how they happen, please forgive her.'

So she too thought I was wrong. That brought more tears to my eyes as she continued.

'I have also reproached this boy and he has shown us that he is sorry; he knows he made a mistake, please find it in your heart to forgive him.'

She concluded by asking my dad not to fire him (as if he was going to). I continued to sob and a cousin seated behind me whispered to me not to cry. I appreciated that because throughout that evening it had felt as if I was on my own trying to defend myself when I had not done anything wrong. My incessant sobs must have begun to irritate my dad because he got up suddenly and stormed towards me.

'Will you shut up right now or I will beat you!'

He had never threatened to beat me before.

'So you have started telling lies, Kebi! You have started telling lies!'

I was desperate.

'I'm not lying, Papa!'

'Shut up! At eight years old you are already telling such elaborate lies?'

He seemed really angry and I desperately wanted him to see that I was telling the truth. Suddenly, I felt breathless and light headed and it scared me but I tried to remain composed. Before I knew it, I fell backwards into the couch and my cousins checked to see if I was alright. My dad was still talking so I tried to refocus my attention on him but my ears were ringing and I was unable to make out what anyone was saying which was even more terrifying. Then suddenly I heard him shout.

'Have you no voice?'

I was confused and looked at my mom since I did not know what my dad was talking about.

He seemed frustrated and angry.

'Can you not speak?' he said.

Although I sensed his frustration, I had missed what he was asking me to speak of. I knew something did not feel right but did not know what it was. My mind had gone blank and I was a little confused; the ringing in my ears had just started to subside when my dad shouted again.

'Do you think it is easy to send all of you to school? And you refuse to do as you are told? George, stand up!'

He stood up and faced my dad who addressed him.

'Today, in the presence of my mother, my aunt and my wife, I will say this only once; from today henceforth, if any of the children disobeys you, you should use a cane and beat them! You follow?'

He mumbled something about not raising spoilt children and stormed out – everyone else slowly dispersed. I lay in bed that night, wondering what had happened to me during the meeting.

Edward said, "Were you able to figure out what happened?"

"I think I nearly fainted."

"Have you had any such experience again?"

"Yes, it actually happened again not long after that. For a few days after the meeting with my dad, George did not say a word to me and instructed Ebot and Junior to stay away from me after school. I ate alone and could not speak to them until my parents came home from work. I felt guilty and spent those afternoons after school alone in my parents' room writing; I documented everything that happened every day. One afternoon as I lay on my mom's carpet writing, George came in and locked the door. He was holding a pestle and lifted a finger to his lips and I sprang to my feet.

'Uncle George, I'm sorry, I didn't mean to report you.'

He pulled me by the ear smiling eerily.

'You went and told Mama that I beat you people.'

'Uncle George, I made a mistake, I will never report you again.'

'Which mistake?' He slapped me, 'Which mistake? Why did you not finish your rice?'

I was confused.

'I said, why did you not finish your rice?' he said again.

I had eaten up all my food that day so I was unsure of what rice he was referring to.

'I finished my food and washed my plate.'

He slapped me again.

'Shut up! You threw your rice in the sink!'

I thought for a moment.

'They were the few grains of rice that were left on my plate...'

'I said shut up your mouth!' He hit me on my left thigh with the pestle.

The weight of it propelled me onto a nearby suitcase and as I screamed he pursed his lips and told me not to make a sound (my grandmother and grand aunt were at the back yard).

'What did Papa say I should do if you don't do what I say?'

I started pleading because only then did I realise what he was trying to do.

'But I finished my food, Uncle George.'

'What did Papa say I should do?'

'He said you should beat us.'

'He said what?'

'He said you should beat us.'

'Okay, show your hand.'

I continued to plead but it fell on deaf ears.

'Look, I don't have time to waste, show your hand!'

I did not stretch out my hand and he got impatient and raised the pestle in the air.

'I will hit your head with this thing,' he threatened.

I stretched out my hand and down came the pestle.

It had been nearly two weeks since he had last beaten me and my body had forgotten what the pain was like – utterly searing. As a result, I did not stretch out my hands as quickly as he instructed so he ended up hitting my back, buttocks and thighs. It was so painful that I felt faint just like I did during the meeting. It was by far the worst beating I'd ever endured but no one noticed because he only hit me on body parts that were concealed by my clothing. I could not even walk properly because I was sore but George threatened to beat me more if anyone noticed I was limping, so I pretended to walk normally whenever I was around others.

Over the next few days, George told me to lie face down and he used *manyanga* oil to massage my back and thighs. But one day he asked me to lie on my back and he rubbed on my groin. I initially thought it odd that anyone would have any interest in touching where someone else's urine came out of but when he said he would never beat me or my brothers again if I let him touch my vagina, I was so glad that I even shared the news with my brothers.

Multifaceted

KEBI WAS ELATED to be at her fourth therapy session.

"I went to lunch with a couple of girlfriends last week and one of them was upset about losing her eighty-something year old grandfather. I felt sad for her but surprised myself when I started crying; my friends were also stunned and said it was the first time they had seen me vulnerable. One of them even remarked that therapy had 'softened' me, which I agree with, to some extent."

Edward was intrigued.

"Would you like to elaborate?"

"Therapy has definitely softened me emotionally; I am not as guarded as I was before and this has allowed me to be more able to connect with others on a deeper level. In a way, it has been liberating because before I started therapy, I found it difficult to allow myself to *really* feel emotion but now I feel the difference within myself. And the fact that I cried so easily about my friend's grandfather's passing indicates that some walls have been broken."

"That is good to hear."

After a long pause, Edward said, "Have you continued to have vivid memories?"

She forced a smile.

"It has been horrible, to be honest. I think talking about George rubbing on my groin in the last session brought back buried memories of horrendous sexual abuse. Just last night, I had the most vivid dream in which I relived a time when he rubbed on my groin everyday and called it *touching*. Although it is painful to think about even right now, at the time I was relieved he was doing it because he stopped beating me. If I did anything which he deemed disobedient, he punished me by *touching* me. At the time, I viewed it as nothing; *all I had to do was lie on my back while he touched himself with one hand and rubbed on my groin with the other*."

She fought back tears but Edward remained silent; he felt it was important for her to get it off her chest.

She continued.

"One afternoon after school, George was having a shower in the *brown toilet* and he called out to me to bring him a bar of soap. I got it and when I got to the door, he asked me to come in. I opened the door slightly and slid my hand in but he pulled me in. I looked away because he was stark naked. He took the soap and laughed.

'Why are turning your head that way? Are you shy?'

I turned to leave and he grabbed hold of my arm and locked the door.

'I want to show you something but you have to be quiet,' he whispered.

I nodded and kept my gaze to the side to avoid looking directly at his penis.

'I will put my tongue like this.'

He stuck out his tongue.

'You have to suck it how you suck sweets.'

I was perplexed but said okay and he stuck out his tongue and noticed my confusion.

'Just pretend you are eating sweets - it's not difficult.'

'But I don't eat sweets,' I said quietly.

I was allergic to sugar and did not eat sweets.

He was getting impatient.

'Does it matter? Pretend that you are sucking sweets, what's wrong with you?'

I was disgusted that he wanted me to suck his tongue but was scared to say no.

'Uncle George, I don't know how to do it,' I whined.

He smiled.

'Come, let me show you, open your mouth.'

I did, with trepidation.

'Open it well.'

I opened it wider.

'Let me see your tongue.'

As I stuck my tongue out, he put his mouth on it and I pulled away instantly.

'You see?' he said victoriously.

He acted as if it was all completely normal.

'It's not hard, now *you* try my own.'

He stuck out his tongue and waited.

I did not know how I was going to get out of it.

'Uncle George, it tastes funny,' I said sheepishly.

'Just try it first.'

I fidgeted with my fingers.

'Just try *na*?' he pressed on.

I continued to fidget and out of the blue, he said I could leave.

The following day after school, I mistakenly burnt my dad's shirt while ironing. I had not been beaten in weeks because I let George *touch* me and I knew that even if he was angry about the burnt shirt, he would not beat me. I was wrong. When I showed him the burn, he slapped me so hard that I fell.

'You are very wicked; I'm going to teach you a lesson!' he said.

He raised his hand to hit me again and I instinctively stepped back, to his annoyance.

'What are you doing, you want to run, where are you running to?'

He reached out and hit the other side of my face but thankfully the back of my hand served as a shield. He pulled me toward himself and shoved the shirt in my face.

'See what you have done! Where is the iron? You want to show me that you can burn clothes? I will show you!'

He pushed me out of his way and stormed towards the front porch where I had been ironing. He continued shouting and as I watched him stomp off, I wondered if other children in the world also went through this. He grabbed the iron and charged toward me holding it out in front of him so I crossed my arms over my face.

'Uncle George, please!'

He pushed me to the floor, placed a foot on my chest and held the iron over my face.

'Uncle George please, I am sorry!' I was too scared to move since I could feel the heat from the iron hovering over my face. On this particular day, there was no other adult at home and whenever this was the case, he behaved more erratically. From the corner of my eye, I caught a glimpse of Ebot and Junior peering through the doorway and George noticed them too.

'Come here!' he shouted.

He pushed Ebot down next to me and with no hesitation he pressed the iron onto Ebot's leg. Ebot screamed so loud I sprang up and pulled him away. We were both hysterical; I could not believe George had burnt him just like that. We were both trembling and wailing as I hugged him tight. The part of his leg that was burnt looked horrific but we were crying so loud that I did not initially hear George shouting for me to go and run Ebot's leg under cold water. He came up to us and said it again and I was about to go with Ebot when George stopped me.

'Yesterday, when I told you to suck my mouth what did you say?'

I was still bewildered by what I had just witnessed and struggled to figure out what he was talking about.

'I said, what did you say?' he shouted.

'Uncle George, I didn't mean to refuse... I'm sorry.'

Meanwhile Ebot began to scream again so George went to check on him. He was away for a couple of minutes and when he returned, he asked me to follow him to our bedroom and he shut the door behind us.

'Did you see what happened to Ebot?'

I nodded.

'It is your fault because you are stubborn.'

'I am sorry, Uncle George, I won't be stubborn anymore.'

I tried to stop crying.

'Do you want me to burn the other leg?'

'No, please, no Uncle George.'

'Hold your ear!'

I did.

'As from today, if you don't want me to burn his leg again, you better do what I say.'

'Yes, I will do anything... please I don't want you to burn him again.'

He looked pleased.

'Come and suck it.'

He sat at the edge of my bed and stuck out his tongue. With tears streaming down my face, I sucked it immediately. He placed one hand on the back of my neck and ordered me to suck harder. Then he began to suck my tongue and when I tried to pull away, he gripped my throat causing me to choke. When he had finished, he told me that was what they called *kissing*.

This became a daily occurrence which I loathed but endured. I learned to get rid of the repulsive taste by washing my mouth with *Omo* washing powder afterwards. Lately, I have been having flashbacks of this and I get nauseous every time.

Edward sighed.

"It sounds horrific."

Kebi nodded.

"It was. And because I never objected to whatever he asked of me, he always took it a step further; what he did next was he tried to get me to suck his penis. I remember telling him it was an odd thing to do since that was *where urine comes from*. And he casually said he had washed it with soap.'

This specific incident happened one night when everyone was in bed. He came and took me from our room to the *brown toilet*. He had a towel with him which he placed on the floor and asked me to kneel on while he sat on the toilet. Although I was shocked and disgusted, I pretended not to have any issue with what he asked so he would have no reason to torment Ebot further. I knelt on the towel but it was soaking wet.

'Uncle George, the towel is wet,' I said.

He checked and saw that it was then he pulled up his trousers and left. While he was gone, I wracked my brain trying to come up with a plan to get out of the situation but did not come up with anything and it made me sad because I felt stuck.

Before I knew it, he tiptoed back in and locked the door. He brought two large towels which he folded and

93

placed over the first one. He sat back down and told me to start. He got annoyed when I did not suck it in the manner in which he wanted and shoved my head downwards onto his penis repeatedly. My infant-sized mouth hurt so much and I got fed up and suddenly closed it.

'Open your mouth!'

He tried not to shout because it was the middle of the night and everyone was asleep.

He continued shoving my head downward but I kept my mouth tightly shut.

'Open it! Don't let me beat you right now!'

In that moment, I really had had enough and did not budge.

'Open your mouth and suck this thing!'

I tried to avoid his penis by moving my head from side to side as he attempted to shove my mouth down onto it. In the scuffle, he grabbed my cornrows and turned my head so I would face him.

'Do you want me to burn Ebot again?'

I almost screamed just thinking of it and shook my head.

'Open your mouth!'

I did and he immediately pushed my head further down causing me choke.

'Suck it!'

I left my mouth open and he began to move his penis back and forth himself. Since I had choked earlier, I moved my head further down suddenly and it made me choke again and I threw up all over him. He pushed me away so hard that I fell on my back.

'I'm sorry, Uncle George... I didn't mean to vomit on you.'

He looked furious.

'See what you have done! Go and sleep!'

I hurried out to another bathroom adjacent to our bedroom, got changed and realised I needed to wash my mouth but remembered the washing powder was in my mom's bathroom. Unfortunately, all I had available to use to clean my mouth was toothpaste. I brushed my mouth over and over with it but the revolting taste of his penis was impossible to get rid of. I eventually gave up and went to bed. But throughout the night, I jumped at the slightest noise because I worried he would return; and when my mom woke us up for school in the morning, it felt as though I had been awake all night.

In school that day, I could not stop thinking about how disgusting it was to have his penis in my mouth. I was so repulsed that I lost my appetite and ate nothing at lunch time. Consequently, the first lesson after lunch, I was very hungry and went to the bathroom to drink water, however, I kept regurgitating because the disgusting taste of his penis was still in my mouth. It was frustrating because I was extremely hungry but could not even swallow water. I sat on the toilet and cried for what seemed like a long time and although I was still hungry after that, I felt relieved because I had not cried so freely in ages.

When we got home from school that day, he seemed to have been eagerly waiting for me, for as soon as we came in through the gate, he asked me to follow him to his room. I had not even greeted my grandmother which was the first thing I did whenever I got home from school. When we got to his room, he locked the door, pulled down his pants and said he wanted us to try it again and that I should let him know beforehand if I felt like vomiting. I immediately burst into tears and he looked surprised.

'What happened?'

'I am hungry and I don't like doing it,' I whimpered.

'You don't like doing it! Come on, bend down and suck this thing before I do something I regret.'

He tried to pull me down to my knees and as I resisted, it turned into a scuffle and he picked up a belt and whipped me once.

'I will beat you! Get up and suck this thing!'

I went down on my knees and he held onto my cornrows - I choked from time to time and he slapped the back of my head to warn me not to vomit. I had been in there for a few minutes when I heard my grandmother call out to me. George pushed me away and pulled up his pants quickly.

'Go outside!' he whispered.

I opened the door and met her in the hallway. She said she had not seen me since I returned from school and had come to look for me. She could not have noticed I was distressed because her eyesight was not great. I went to the backyard with her and even got Ebot and Junior to join us and we ate together. At some point, she asked me to go and get changed out of my uniform but I did not leave her side. I tried to stay with her for as long as possible but after a while, George came and called for me.

I fought back tears as I went with him because he got angry if he saw you crying; it was too late because as I stepped into his room, he saw that I was crying and pulled me by the ear.

'What are you crying for?'

Before I could respond, he whacked my arm with something that felt like metal and when I screamed he quickly put a finger to his lips.

He sat down and forced himself into my mouth again scolding at me to do it properly.

In my eight-year old mind, I figured if I didn't do it properly he would hopefully stop asking me to do it altogether. So I geared myself and bit down on his penis with all my might. He screamed so loud my ears were ringing. I still remember the feeling of his flesh in my teeth – that was how hard I bit him.

'Get out of here, you idiot!' he screamed.

I went to my room and cried.

Kebi noticed Edward was wiping tears away.

"I am sorry I made you cry."

"Please, don't apologise... what you went through is utterly despicable," he dabbed his eyes with tissue.

Exasperated, she shook her head and forced a smile and spoke slowly.

"I don't know how to get rid of these memories, Edward, so I am hoping you can help me. They are there when I wake up and they are there when I go to sleep at night. They are there when I am in the train, in the bus, in the shower and even in noisy environments... they pop up sporadically and leave me so mentally drained. And now this entire situation has begun to affect my kids because I am never really present when I am with them. I have no idea how to get rid of these memories in my head. I really need your help."

Knee-Deep

AT HER PREVIOUS SESSION she learned about dealing with painful memories and flashbacks. Edward explained that flashbacks were useful since they were the brain's way of dealing with past trauma in order to provide necessary healing. With this in mind, Kebi's attitude toward dealing with them changed remarkably; she went from being overwhelmed to confident when they occurred. Edward introduced her to the use of positive coping statements to deal with flashbacks effectively. For instance, she was once at the park with her kids when her three year old son fell over and started to cry. The sound of him crying triggered a flashback of an incident (with George) in which her three year old brother, Junior was held upside down from his leg and beaten with a shoe. At the time, when Kebi begged George to stop beating him, he said he would only stop if she let him *touch* her. She agreed and he let Junior go instantly. She was emotional as she recalled this incident whilst consoling her son at the park; but she knew she had to pull herself together for the sake of her kids. She therefore used positive coping statements she had learned in therapy.

She said, *'This is just a bad memory, it hurts to think about it but it is in the past, I am not there anymore and neither is Junior. No one can hurt us now. It is just a memory and it shall pass.'*

And because she truly believed what she had said, it eventually went away and she continued playing with her kids.

As she recounted this at her next therapy session, Edward was pleased to hear she had been managing the flashbacks well.

"It is your dedication that has facilitated the progress you have made."

"Thank you," she smiled.

Edward cleared his throat.

"Is there anything specific you would like to talk about?"

Kebi thought the question was ironic since she *really* wanted to talk to him about everything else that happened with George and the extreme ways in which she was affected by them. She found it freeing to talk with a professional who had no personal ties to her – it was easier talking to him than to friends and family – including her husband, Ofe. She had never told anyone *everything* that happened; she did not think anyone could withstand it. Edward had already helped her so much with his knowledge, insight and perspectives that the prospect of gaining more knowledge that could potentially turn her life around was inviting.

"Definitely," she said, "I would like to continue narrating the events that happened after the penis-biting incident."

Edward appeared taken aback.

"Oh okay, was that where we stopped last week?"

"Yes, I only remembered because I jotted it down," she smiled.

"Okay, whenever you are ready..."

She took a deep breath.

"So... after the penis-biting incident, George never asked me to suck it again but he called me to his room and said he was going to show me how to do it differently. He asked me to lie on my stomach. When I did, he spat on his palm, rubbed it on his penis, spat on his palm again and rubbed it on my thighs. Then he placed his penis between my thighs and began to thrust but without penetration."

She paused and forced a smile.

Edward said, "Once again, I am so sorry you went through that... did you say there was no penetration in that instance?"

"Yeah, there was none. He thrust his penis between my thighs to make himself ejaculate but it never went near my vagina. He also called this *touching*, and by the time I was nine years old, he was doing it a few times a day even when there were people at home. It was like an addiction. When there people around, he did everything to get my attention; he mostly touched the wall or any surface with the palm of his hand and that was my signal to come with him. If I did not go, he recorded it as a round of beatings. Because I knew I was supposed to look out for his signal, I never looked his way when he was around... I spent my days pretending to be engrossed in *anything* simply so as not

103

to look his way. It was a hellish kind of life because I was always on the lookout for him. When he realised it was challenging to get my attention, he took it a step further and started to speak up in order to get my attention."

"How did he do this?"

"By saying the word '*touching*' out loud. I'll give you an example; I was once hanging out with my cousins and he wanted to me to come with him so he came and sat with us. After a while, he said, 'Kebi, help me spell *towel*.' I spelled it without looking at him because I knew what he was up to. From the corner of my eye, I could see him gently patting the wall but I pretended not to notice. Moments later, he asked me to spell the word '*touching*' and he continued to touch the wall. Everyone else was oblivious to what was going on and they continued their conversations and as I spelled '*touching*', he patted the wall continuously but I acted as if I had not noticed."

He said, 'What did you just spell?'

'Touching,' I said.

'And what am I doing now?'

'Touching the wall?'

I continued to act none the wiser.

He seemed frustrated at some point and gave me a threatening look as he walked out... I knew I had to go with him."

Kebi paused and started to cry.

"He was just a complete asshole, you know... a sick bastard who jacked up my childhood," she wept.

Edward placed another box of tissues next to her.

"Thank you," she smiled as she dried her eyes. "You'll soon have to start charging me for these boxes of tissues."

They both smiled then she regrouped and continued.

"He made himself ejaculate at least twice a day by rubbing his penis on my thighs. The first time he raped me vaginally was when he got mad because I mistakenly added too much salt to a pot of rice. I was nine at the time and from that day on, the number of times he came to me for sex increased per day."

Kebi was overcome with emotion and sobbed for a little while, as Edward remained silent.

"Kebi," he finally said calmly, "We can stop the session now if it is a bit much for you... you don't have to talk about all of it today."

Resting her face in her hands, she remained silent for a while then reached into her bag for a bottle of water.

"I will be okay... I know I will. It is just that I have never spoken about these things to anyone before... so all of it is still very raw."

Edward forced a smile as Kebi took a sip of water.

She stared at the wall blankly for a while.

Suddenly, she said, "You know what? You're right, I'll go home now."

Night

FOR AS LONG AS SHE COULD REMEMBER, Kebi had suffered from insomnia. She was so accustomed to it that she never once thought to seek professional help. It worsened when she started therapy so she mentioned it to Edward, hoping for some guidance on how to ameliorate it.

"How old were you when you first started having trouble sleeping?" Edward asked.

"I was about nine years old."

"Do you think there might be any association between the insomnia and your abuse?"

"I know it is definitely linked to my abuse," she said, "George had been abusing me during the day as well as at night and I became a light sleeper as a result. But it got worse after an attempted burglary at our house. Although the burglars were unable to gain access into the main house, the mere fact that they had attempted to break in terrified me and from that day on, I found it even more difficult to fall asleep at night. Luckily, my dad decided to further secure the rooms by ensuring every door had a key. This meant we finally had a key to our bedroom door and locked it every night when we went to bed. The bonus for me was that it stopped George from coming to me at night. However, after a few nights of not having him come, he was heard screaming from outside my parents' bedroom window one night, claiming to have heard screams for help from our bedroom. They rushed over shouting for us to open the door and when we eventually did, they found that none of us had shouted for help. But after that, George suggested that my dad leave our room key outside our door so it will be easier for an adult to get to us in case of an emergency."

Edward shook his head as Kebi continued.

"To think that he went to such extreme lengths to be able to have sex with me, a nine year old child."

She paused then continued.

108

"Do you know what I learned from this specific incident? A paedophile will do anything to facilitate their access to a child."

Edward sighed.

"Did your dad take his suggestion to leave the keys outside your door?"

"Yep..."

Kebi forced a smile.

"For the few days when we locked our bedroom door from inside, it must have stirred up a lot of anxiety in him to know that he would no longer be able to access me easily at night."

She paused to recollect her thoughts.

"On the first night of having our keys outside the door, I heard someone trying to come in. Fortunately, the keys made such a loud noise that my mom came out to see what was going on. By the time she got there, the person was gone. I knew it was George. The following night he tried to come in again and after a long struggle he succeeded in entering the room without the keys jangling. In the darkness, I watched as he approached my bed stealthily and as usual, I pretended to be fast asleep in order to make it more

109

challenging for him to rape me (my efforts never paid off but I still tried). What normally happened was, he pinched me until I woke up then I followed him to the *brown toilet* where he raped me. On this specific night, instead of pinching me, he slid his arms around me to lift me off my bed. In my nine-year old mind, I thought if I was completely stiff, I would be too heavy for him to carry. So I stiffened my bum, thighs, arms and even tightened my fists but he still lifted me off my bed. And for the first time ever, he raped me on the floor of our bedroom with my brothers asleep."

She continued.

"The very next night, he came to the room again and he neither pinched me nor did he lift me off my bed; instead, he slid his hand underneath my nightdress. I took a deep breath and screamed at the top of my lungs. 'Papa! There's someone in our room!'

I continued to shout as he staggered backwards and within seconds, my mom was there."

She looked shaken.

'What happened?' she said.

George was at the door next to her but I avoided his gaze as I spoke to her.

'There was someone in the room.'

Just then my dad pushed his way past both of them and came to my bedside.

'Kebi, what happened?'

He looked extremely worried and examined my cheeks and chin as though in search of answers.

'Someone was in our room,' I said again.

He gave a deep sigh of relief.

'I think you just had a bad dream.'

My mom looked at George.

'George, how did you get here so quickly?' she said.

'I was on my way to the toilet then I heard her shouting so I came in then you too came in. I think she was just dreaming,' he chuckled.

My dad said, 'Okay, Kebi, you children should go back to sleep... you had a bad dream. Mama, switch off the light so they can go back to sleep.'

He said goodnight and he and George left the room as my mom stood in the doorway waiting for us to settle into our beds so she could switch off the light. George went past her then he turned and looked at me.

He mouthed, 'You will see,' and walked off.

My mom said good night and shut the door. I cried quietly all night since I knew what awaited me the next day. I was mad at myself for screaming too soon. I wished I had waited until he was on top of me before screaming. I had wanted to execute this plan for months and when I finally did, it went terribly wrong. For the first time ever, I wished God would take my life so I would not experience George's wrath.

The following day, I struggled to focus in class; I specifically remember being asked to correct someone's misspelling of 'giraffe' (I was good at spellings) but I stood up and spelled it with one 'f'.

The teacher said, 'Wrong, try again.'

I spelled it in exactly the same way and the class laughed. The teacher asked if I knew why everyone was laughing and I could not figure out why until someone else spelled it correctly. My mind was preoccupied with what awaited me at home after school. I wished I did not have to go home and began to consider ways in which to make that happen. I finally made up my mind to sneak out of school during break-time – I was going to leave through the school gate and run away so no one would ever find me. Break-time finally came and I

112

went to the gate only to find that it was locked; I stood there and cried. As home-time drew near, I became more distressed since I still had no plausible explanation to give George for the night before.

When we pulled up to our house after school (we were carpooled by a family friend's driver), George promptly appeared at the gate smiling warmly as he let us in. He held the gate open while exchanging pleasantries with the driver and as I walked in, I noticed the pestle carefully leaned against a side wall. I quickly pushed Ebot and Junior further into the house and told them not to come out no matter what. As they hurried away, I heard George say goodbye to the driver and lock the gate.

'The queen is back from school!' he said mockingly, 'Come here, you this idiot!'

He grabbed the pestle and swung it onto my chest so hard that I fell down. I immediately started crying as I pressed where it hurt. He picked me up from my ribs and flung me against the wall shouting.

'You think you can fool me?'

My chest was throbbing and I was certain my ribs were broken but despite my supplications, he kicked, dragged and punched me on my back, chest and midriff. I had never felt such intense pain in my life but I took deep breaths and tried not to cry in the hope that he would have mercy on me if I did not cry. He continued to shout and said I knew it was him who was in the room the night before. He said he was going to show me that I had chosen the wrong person to play games with and that I would remember this lesson for the rest of my life. He pointed at my uniform.

'Move this thing!'

Seated on the floor, I undressed quickly.

'Take off the pant!'

As I did, I continued to plead.

'I made a mistake... I didn't know it was you who was in the room, I thought it was a thief.'

'You are lying... show your hand!'

I held out my hand and the pestle came down hard. How my flesh and bones remained intact, I have no idea. I wailed as he whipped my palms continuously until he lost his grip and the pestle fell on the floor and rolled away.

'Uncle George, I am begging you please, I'm sorry.'

'Lie down!'

114

When I did, he picked up a tree branch and whipped my bum, instructing me to count as he whipped. I don't remember what number I had counted to, but I was completely depleted and could no longer withstand the pain. I thought about my brothers and imagined us running around, tickling each other and laughing. It was heart-warming to see them smiling (in my mind). For a brief moment, I slipped back into cognizance and realised he was still beating me. Then I snapped out and felt nothing.

At least a couple of weeks went by and one day, as I helped my mom tidy the backyard she called me over and lifted my blouse up. She was horrified at what she saw.

'What is this? What happened to your back?'

I said, 'Where?'

'All these marks on your back.'

'I fell in school.'

'You fell in school how? Look at these marks!' She gasped as she pulled my blouse further up and examined my arms and my stomach.

'What did you fall from?'

'The monkey bar.'

She seemed suspicious as she stared at me.

'You fell from a monkey bar?'

I nodded.

'How high is this monkey bar that you would get marks like these?'

'Does this hurt?'

I shook my head.

You fell so badly and the school did not even tell me? They will get it hot from me tomorrow!'

She asked to know when it happened and whom I had reported it to; I lied that I had told my teacher. That night, I could hardly sleep because I had lied about my teacher and was worried about the repercussions.

"I'm sorry you had to go through that," Edward said.

"Thank you."

"What happened when your mom went to your teacher then?"

Kebi shrugged.

"I honestly don't know what happened. My teacher never asked me about it so... "

"Did your mom talk to you about it again?"

"She didn't *talk* about it but she examined my back and asked how I was feeling..."

"What about George... how was he with you and your brothers after that?"

"As usual, he showed remorse and even helped massage my back a few times but that was his pattern; he hurt us, showed remorse and recounted a sob story about his family's poverty. He had me exactly where he wanted and knew I would not report him to my parents because I felt bad for him. After that particular incident, he did not beat any of us for what felt like a very long time and during that time I tried to do better with cooking and cleaning so as not to get beaten again."

"Did that help?"

"It did for a while until he got really annoyed one day; I actually narrated this to my husband just the other day. We had been waiting for our food for a very long time one day, and were hungry; whenever George went to the kitchen to check on the food that was cooking, Ebot and I sneakily drank water from the tap at the backyard. We did this for a while and Ebot's stomach became engorged; I laughed so much because his stomach was so big and he drank more to make me laugh more. Soon after, the food was ready and George called us in for lunch but as soon as I took the first spoon of rice, I knew I would not be able to eat any more because of how full I was (from the water I had drunk). I looked over at Ebot and his mouth was also stuffed with food he could barely chew. Within moments, George started threatening to beat us if we did not eat quickly and he went to the kitchen to get the pestle. When he was gone, I told Ebot to try not to vomit, which was something we did frequently because George made us eat way too much food. And every time we vomited, he raped me as punishment."

Edward uncrossed his legs as he listened on.

He returned and waved the pestle around a few times while hurling threats at us. In an attempt to show him I was eating progressively, I scooped more spoons of rice into my mouth but could hardly breathe let alone chew. Ebot also struggled and tears ran down his ballooning cheeks as I telepathically willed him to hang in there. But suddenly, everything gushed out of his mouth and as if on cue, I too disgorged the contents of my stomach.

I saw (and heard) the pestle land on Ebot's back and he screamed and jumped up from the table. He was hit so hard that the pestle rolled down the stairs and George stormed after it shouting.

'I will break somebody's back today!'

I quickly ducked under the table and with both hands, I scooped up vomited rice from the floor and put it in my plate then hurried back up from under the table. Ebot sobbed quietly as he sat back down and I noticed he still had a lot of food in his plate. Promptly, I shifted about half of it into my plate as George climbed back up the stairs. I had much food in my plate but did not care because I knew Ebot would be able to finish what was left in his plate. George noticed the small amount of food in his plate and immediately looked on the floor.

'When you finish, eat the food that is on the floor!'

He always made us eat regurgitated food from the floor but this time there was none really since I had scooped it up, so he let Ebot leave the table when he finished eating minutes later.

"Where was Junior?" Edward asked.

"He was not present during this incident but I don't remember exactly where he was. It was always comforting whenever he and Ebot were not in the vicinity when George was angry."

He stood watching me struggle to get through nearly a quarter of the food in my plate.

'What should I do to you if you don't finish that food?' he asked.

'I don't know,' I said with a mouth full of food.

'You don't know eh? Go and wait for me in the toilet.'

Listen

DURING THE SEVENTH SESSION, Kebi discussed her guilt.

"When I turned ten, my dad started talking about secondary schools to apply to in preparation for the following academic year. My ordeal was ongoing so I was thrilled at the prospect of leaving it all behind and going away to boarding school; but I felt guilty about having to leave Ebot and Junior at home with George. At the time, I had become snappy toward him and this resulted in one too many beatings on them; for instance, he once asked me to do a chore and peevishly, I said I would do it later because I was tired. He scolded me and said if I did not do it immediately, I would regret it; I remained seated and said nothing.

Seemingly infuriated that I had ignored him, he yanked me up and said, 'Am I not talking to you?'

121

'Leave me alone!' I retorted, 'I have been cleaning the house since I came back from school and you, the house boy, are sitting here doing nothing.'

He slapped me and I smiled in his face to show him I was not intimidated. He then charged purposefully out of the living room and moments later, came in dragging Junior. He flung him viciously across the room onto the sofa and I ran over and put my arms around him as he cried. George scolded me to leave him alone but I ignored him. He repeatedly shouted at him to shut up which made him cry more so he picked up a shoe and aimed it at him; luckily, my arm got in the way and it missed his head. Annoyed, George grabbed my arm and jerked it up behind my back, forcing me to let go of Junior.

'You better do what I say or you will cry,' he said.

I tried to wriggle out of his grasp but he jerked my arm further up behind my back; I screamed from the pain and he let go but continued shouting at me.

'Press his head!' he scolded.

He wanted me to pin Junior face down on the sofa so he could whip him; I welled up with tears as I gently turned him into position. Still sobbing, Junior turned to look at me whilst my hand was on his back and George noticed I was not really holding him down.

'Hold him with power!' he shouted.

Again, I pretended to pin him down while Junior wailed. George whipped him three times on his bare bottom and sent him to our room. Before he ran off, I pulled up his trousers and whispered to him to stay in the room. But I carried a lot of guilt over the years for causing him to be beaten like that on that day.

Edward paused.

"What do you mean?"

"With me holding him face down while George beat him," Kebi pursed her lips.

"I can't begin to imagine what that must have felt like," said Edward.

"It was horrible... the more I vowed not to do anything to make my brothers get beaten up, the snappier I was with George and the more drastic the punishments became."

"How did it all come to an end?"

She fought back tears as she thought back to how it ended.

One night when he came to me, I quite unexpectedly told him he could not touch me because I was in pain – I had persistent vaginal pain. He tried to forcibly pull me out of bed but I fought him off and surprisingly, he left me alone.

I was eating in the kitchen when he brought it up the next day; I showed no remorse and overtly ignored him by humming to myself. He took an empty jute bag (the big brown ones used as sacks for rice) and suddenly grabbed my arm and dragged me ferociously across the rough cement floor and out to the front yard. Unfortunately, when we got there Ebot and Junior were playing in the sand so he let go of me, snatched Ebot and forced him into the sack while I fought and begged him to put me inside instead. Ebot wailed and wriggled but George ignored both our pleas and tied the sack up angrily; then he raced to the back yard and flung the sack over the fence as if he was tossing a ball.

I screamed and headed for the gate running as fast as I could. On the other side of the fence was an extensive piece of stony, neglected farm land which grew plantains, guavas and cassava. As I bolted towards

124

the farm land crying, I prayed that Ebot had not landed on his head; I prayed he was not bleeding. I felt guilty to have once again caused him pain.

I got to the periphery of the farm land and crawled across a muddy trench to get inside; rapidly scrambling on all fours through the dirt and thorny bushes I started looking for the brown sack. I shouted out Ebot's name and did not hear anything so I continued crawling; it was a vast piece of land on a slope so I held on to branches and bushes to keep me from tumbling down. I worked my way through quickly but I could not find the sack. I stopped to listen but heard nothing and I started to panic and called his name again when I heard him crying towards the far right but when I tried to crawl under another thorny bush, my corn-rows got stuck. I pulled and tugged at the branches but they were extremely prickly; just then Ebot screamed louder, so I forced my head through, gravely bruising my head. It stung badly but I needed to get to him. I was scared he might die.

I found the sack at the base of a tree but when I got to it, I found that it was tightly knotted and I could not undo it. Ebot was terrified and screamed nonstop as I continued trying to unknot it. I reassured him I would open it even though I had no idea how, then I began to bite into the side of the sack and soon created a small hole which I managed to rip open. It was arduous but because Ebot was a small seven year-old, he forced his way out through the tiny hole. He hugged me tight and we cried – I had never been so overwhelmed with guilt than in that moment. I looked up at our fence and realised the sack had not rolled too far down from where it landed but was diverted by the bushes. Luckily, the shrubs and weeds had prevented him from rolling further down the slope. Then I remembered we had to return home so I took his hand.

'Come, let's go.'

As we hurried back up the slope, I noticed he was still crying so I stopped and dried his eyes with his T-shirt.

'Don't cry or else he will beat us again.'

'Okay,' he took a deep breath and attempted to stop crying.

George was waiting at the gate with his hands behind his back and our neighbours were out on their front porch deep in conversation - they did not notice us. No sooner had we gone in through the gate, did I drop to my knees pulling Ebot down next to me.

'Uncle George we are sorry, we won't do it again,' I said. He locked the gate carefully and turned to me almost with an air of victory and spoke calmly.

'You are sorry eh? So what will you do? Will you let me touch?'

'Yes.'

'Remove your clothes.'

It was odd because he had never told me to take off my clothes in front of anyone before but I obeyed.

'Go and wait for me inside,' he said.

Ebot and I ran to our bedroom where we found Junior seated quietly on my bed - I was so relieved to see him unhurt. Before leaving them to go and wait for George in the bathroom, I reminded them to stay in the room no matter what. They said yes in unison and as they looked at me, it broke my heart to see how sad they were. In that moment especially, I blamed myself for everything; I had repeatedly told them not to tell anyone anything. But just then, I felt like I needed to put an end to it. I was tired of seeing them sad, tired of being beaten, tired of being touched, tired of being sore. I shut the door and went out to George.

As soon as I saw him, I began to shout - I told him I had had enough of him beating us and touching me every day. I said I would never let him touch me again and if he did, he would have to kill me first.

'Shut your mouth!'

He tried to keep his voice down, I guessed, so my neighbours would not hear.

'I will not shut up, Uncle George! I won't shut up! Ebot and Junior are sad! We are living like prisoners in our own house! Why don't you leave us alone and go and beat your age mates! You will never touch me again! You can beat me all you want but I will not let you touch me!'

He smashed his hand across my face and I fell. I held my face but continued shouting at the top of my voice.

'Slap me again if you want but I will not stand here and let you beat me! My own father has never laid a finger on me, but you... a stinking houseboy! You beat me every day! Every single day! Leave us alone!'

I got up and started walking away (I still had no clothes on) but he caught up with me and kicked me in the back telling me to shut up. I almost tripped but kept going, a bit faster. He shouted at me to stop but I did not then I saw him striding towards me so I began to run. I ran to the gate, unlocked it and ran to a neighbour's house.

I had seen her outside earlier so I screamed out to her as I ran into her house.

'Tata Marie, Uncle George is about to beat me!'

Tata Marie and my mom were friends and she was always nice to us. She came out exclaiming in her usual high-pitched voice.

'What is happening, where are your clothes, why are you naked?'

She covered me with a table cloth she happened to be holding and led me further into her house. I knew George would turn up almost immediately since he was at my heels so I quickly told Tata Marie that he had been beating us for years and that he was about to beat me again – she asked if my mom was aware he had been beating us and I said she was. She exclaimed and looked up and there he was behind me.

'George, what is the meaning of this rubbish?" she exclaimed, "Why would you beat her until her head bleeds like this?'

She sounded very angry as she examined the cuts on my forehead.

'Aunty, she is very stubborn and opposes everything I say...'

'It's a lie, Tata Marie!' I interjected, 'he tells lies and Papa tells him to beat us for no reason!'

She looked confused.

'Your father asked him to beat you?'

'Yes, he did.'

'Unbelievable,' she retorted.

George chimed in.

'Aunty, I just follow their father's instructions and he says I should beat them when they are stubborn.'

She snapped.

'That doesn't mean you should beat them and strip them naked as if they are thieves! This is not normal! They are children; you can correct children without treating them like animals.'

George suddenly softened and changed his tune.

'Aunty, I'm sorry I don't mean to beat them like that but sometimes they are very naughty and there is no other way to get them to do what they have to do.'

'Like what?' she asked.

'Like eating their food.'

'So you beat a child because they don't want to eat their food... why not wait for their mother to come home and you tell her that they refused to eat?'

He remained silent as she went on.

'It is not your place to beat them to this extent.'

I was happy she was telling him off and surprisingly, he seemed to be sincerely sorry.

'I have heard, Aunty.'

He almost sounded child-like as she continued to rain advice on him.

'Even if their father tells you to beat them, please, remember that they are children not adults, don't use such force on them, please.'

He apologised again then reached for my hand but I did not budge. Instead, I whispered to Tata Marie that he might still be upset with me but she instantly slammed the idea.

131

'No, go with him, he will not do anything to you. I have spoken to you haven't I, George?'

'Yes, Aunty.'

'And you will not beat them with so much force anymore right?'

'Yes, Aunty.'

'Okay, Kebi don't worry about it. Go home and try to be a good girl from now on so you don't get beaten. If you choose to be stubborn, it is up to you - I cannot tell your parents to stop beating you if you are stubborn because as you already know, I beat my own children when they are naughty.'

She let me go home with the cloth wrapped around me and George thanked her as we left. Our house was literally next door; he said nothing as we walked along to our gate. Once we were inside, he calmly told me to go and wait for him in his room because he wanted to talk to me about what had happened. I waited there and not long after, he came in with a bunch of my father's ties and asked me to sit on his bed. When I did, he carefully wrapped a tie around my wrist then around a bedpost and as he tightened it, I told him it hurt but he ignored me. He then went to the other side of the bed, reached across and pulled me over – I knew it was not a good sign since he had a smile plastered on his face but was not saying anything. He tied my left hand to the opposite bed post and pulled the cloth off me.

'Uncle George,' I pleaded, 'I will never report you again... I made a mistake.'

He stood opposite me and casually took off his clothes.

'So you will not report me again eh?'

'I will never report you again, please Uncle George, I made a mistake and I'm sorry for telling Tata Marie.'

While I was speaking, he sat next to me at the edge of the bed, still smiling.

'Have you finished?'

I nodded.

'You are a child so I forgive you, you hear?'

I nodded and thanked him then he continued.

'But when somebody does something very bad, they have to be punished; I will give you your punishment so you will never ever talk to me with that big mouth again.'

He got on top of me and raped me anally.

I screamed for him to stop but he kept going. I fought with my head, my legs and my teeth. I bit him all over until he bled but he did not stop. He hit me repeatedly and pinned me down to stop me from head-butting and wriggling. It was the worst pain I had ever experienced. He continued to pound into me with more and more rage for what seemed like a very long time. In that moment, I cried out for God to take my life so I would no longer feel. And gradually, I left my body and felt nothing.

I have no recollection of what happened thereafter so I think I might have passed out but I do not know for sure.

For the next few weeks, I did not go to school. I was sick, lost my hearing in one ear and was admitted into hospital where my mom stayed with me. When we returned home, my mom and grand aunt nursed me daily with herbal treatments whereby I sat over a boiling pot of fever grass herbs mixed with pawpaw, cocoyam and plantain leaves with a large blanket covered over me. It was extremely hot and confined and although I did not like it, I endured it because they said it would give me strength. They also gave me massages twice a day *to heal my aching joints* but I did not know if they knew what had actually happened to me. No one spoke about it. No one asked me anything. But even if they had asked, I would have said nothing because I had finally learnt my lesson with regards to George: to keep my mouth shut.

After that incident, George never beat us again but he continued to rape me. I became even more withdrawn than before and spoke very little. Family members noticed my reticence and erroneously assumed it was because I was *growing up*.

Recluse

AT THE NEXT SESSION, Edward addressed the after-effects of child abuse.

"From what I have gathered, you were surrounded by a lot of power and submissiveness during your childhood; as a result, you learned subservience from an early age. Behaviours that we become accustomed to when we are young often stay with us in adulthood; this may be the reason why today you find yourself obeying others unquestioningly."

Kebi agreed.

"I was definitely accustomed to submissiveness."

"Unfortunately, being submissive is common among victims of child abuse and has a lot to do with the need to gain other people's approval due to a lack of confidence in their own worth."

Kebi paused as she let his words sink in then she nodded.

"Isn't that low self-esteem?" she asked.

"It is."

She remembered something.

"A few weeks ago, a friend of mine suggested I might be suffering from low self-esteem when I told her about some issues I was having. After our conversation, I read up on it and was a bit confused; I read that people with low self-esteem generally do not think positively of themselves and do not speak up if they are being mistreated. I know I never speak up no matter how unpleasant my situation is but I have never thought negatively or worthlessly of myself, so it made me wonder if I truly have low self-esteem or if I'm confusing it with something else."

Edward explained.

"You are absolutely right in your thinking. Self-esteem is a word that is used to describe a person's overall self-worth; that is, how they value themselves. It covers a broad spectrum and an individual who lacks self-esteem would be one who views themselves as totally worthless (among other things) while one with too much self-esteem has an exaggerated sense of self-worth."

Kebi listened attentively and jotted as he explained.

She said, "So, a person with too much self-esteem acts somewhat like a narcissist?"

"Precisely."

As he explained further, she sketched a vertical scale on her notepad and annotated it as she asked further questions, while trying to fully grasp his explanations.

Edward explained further.

"Someone at the bottom of the self-esteem spectrum would likely lack self-worth or self-love, think negatively of themselves and their life, and allow people to mistreat them."

Kebi continued jotting as he went on.

"On the other hand, a person at the top end has an over-inflated view of themselves and is sometimes said to have a *God complex*. The ideal area to be on the spectrum is somewhere in the middle."

Kebi added, "Because there is a good balance in the middle?"

"Correct."

She paused to think about it.

"So using the self-esteem spectrum, would you say I am more towards the lower end than the middle?"

He chose his words carefully.

"Not everyone with low self-esteem exhibits the same traits; some people self-harm while others would not dare to. The characteristics a person displays determine where they fall on the self-esteem spectrum. I believe *you* have a healthy level of self-esteem which you could make a little healthier by starting to view yourself as worthy of better..."

Kebi nodded and jotted quickly as Edward continued.

"To achieve this, the main aspect to focus on is your conditioning."

Kebi thought for a moment.

"How the hell do I go about changing my conditioning?" she chuckled.

"By being open and by allowing yourself to be present in experiencing new things, exploring different ways of doing things and even listening to people whom you would never normally listen to."

Kebi noted those.

"You make it sound easy," she said.

He smiled.

"It is not. It takes lots of commitment."

"I'm definitely up for the challenge; I don't want to go through life having low self-esteem... how sad would that be?" she smiled.

Edward smiled too.

"Were there other aspects that incited your friend to come to the conclusion that you might have low self-esteem?"

"The main reason why she said so was because of my inability to speak up when I'm in unpleasant situations but another reason was that I get extremely uncomfortable when I am in the midst of people having a conversation. Even when they are people I know, I get nervous for no apparent reason."

Edward sighed.

"When you think back to such moments; what are you most nervous about?"

She paused to think about it.

"Saying something stupid," she smiled.

Edward explained.

"When people worry about the possibility of saying something stupid, it can be either due to a lack of confidence or a belief that others in the group are smarter or more knowledgeable about the topic of discussion."

He paused to let Kebi finish jotting.

"Does that make any sense?" he asked.

"It does... everything you just said totally applies to me."

She paused.

"Can I ask a question?"

"Fire away..."

"If this is the case, why do I not get nervous during one-to-one conversations in which I am not familiar with the topic being discussed?"

"I'll ask you a question before I explain?" he said.

"Okay."

"Were you shy when you were younger?"

"I would not say I was shy; I was very attentive and that sometimes came across as shyness. I was not super talkative but definitely not shy."

Once again, he paced himself so she would not miss any information.

"To answer your question, I think your anxiety in group conversations stems partly from your childhood in which you were criticized and scrutinized extensively.

Although you are naturally comfortable speaking, when there is a group of people, you tend to worry about being scrutinized by many people at the same time and this makes you self-conscious. How do you feel in a six or seven-person conversation compared to a three-person conversation?"

"I am perfectly fine in a three-person conversation – no nerves whatsoever... when it gets to about five people is when I start sweating but ironically, when I was at university, I gave lots of presentations and was never nervous when talking to a room full of people."

Edward nodded.

"That's probably because you rehearsed your presentation and knew exactly what to say; so despite the fact that you were standing in front of say a hundred students giving a presentation, you were confident because it had been rehearsed and that eliminated any anxiety."

Kebi nodded and took a few more notes.

"That makes so much sense... I really appreciate your clear explanations, Edward."

He smiled as she went on.

"You have shed light on things about me which I did not particularly like but did not understand and would never have attributed to my abuse. With this newfound awareness and knowledge, especially pertaining to my abuse, I am ready to put in the work to get rid of everything that is hindering me from being my best self; the submissiveness, lack of confidence and self-esteem. I know it will be a lot of work but I need to make a change for my sake and that of my family. Apart from changing my conditioning, which I believe is a great starting point, what else can I do to change all of it?"

Edward sat up and cleared his throat.

"I would say, start by trying to view everyone as your equal."

Kebi nodded.

He went on.

"No one is more superior until you allow them to be."

He paused to let her finish writing.

She looked up.

"You hit the nail on the head with that because I find that I spontaneously 'shrink' when I am in the midst of certain people."

Edward looked a bit uncertain.

"Would you kindly explain what you mean?"

"What I mean is, when I am around certain people, without conscious thought or attention, I instantly feel less than them."

Edward seemed to understand.

"How does this manifest itself?"

"I feel intimidated so I literally remain silent since it is the safest thing for me to do in that situation. But if I *have* to say something, I keep it very brief."

"Why do you think you keep it brief?"

Kebi chuckled.

"Because I don't want to say the wrong thing and look stupid."

Edward seemed to follow what she was saying.

He said, "This comes back to what I said earlier regarding viewing everyone as your equal. When you place someone at a higher level than yourself, you feel like you have to be mindful of what you say when you are around them, in order not to be viewed as stupid."

Kebi listened closely as he explained.

"It will take time and some practice because it is not always easy to unlearn childhood habits. It is possible but will take time."

Kebi felt empowered.

"Basically, what you're saying is I just need to go for it and say whatever I want to say."

"Precisely," he added, "I have an exercise for you... let's assume you found yourself in the same situation with the patient with whom you had a run-in; what would you do differently?"

"I would definitely speak up much sooner."

"What would you say in response to him complimenting your physical appearance?"

Kebi felt put on the spot and could not think of what to say.

"I don't know... even now, I can't think of what to say, it's so annoying," she grinned.

"It's okay, it takes practice..."

Kebi interjected.

"Wait, I've got one..."

"Okay?"

"If he complimented me on my appearance I would smile and say, '*Thank you, but let's get on with the tests so we can get you sorted out quickly.*' Yeah, I would say something along those lines."

Edward said, "That sounds pretty good – it's polite, professional and to the point."

Kebi smiled as he went on.

"Whatever situation you find yourself in, if you ever feel uncomfortable, step away from it to give yourself time to think through what you want to say."

"Right, so using my situation with the patient, I could have simply walked out sooner and it wouldn't have escalated to the point it did."

Edward nodded as she continued.

"In hindsight, I believe I did not want the patient to know that I was offended by his words... I think that was partly why I endured it... just like I endured my childhood abuse in silence."

"Correct."

Kebi paused and reflected on how oblivious she had been to the impact her abuse had had on her for most of her life.

"I like therapy," she sighed.

Edward smiled.

"It is useful. It allows you to see things from a different perspective."

"I agree, I don't think I would have ever realised how impactful my childhood abuse was, on something as simple as my interaction with others."

Edward spoke slowly.

"As we mentioned earlier, it's also about self-confidence. Going through childhood abuse often strips away self-confidence amongst many other things. Regaining it is not always easy but is not impossible. You have to view yourself as worthy of all the qualities you possess and start from there."

She jotted as he spoke.

He continued, "Building self-confidence can even help prevent future assaults..."

"You mean because you learn to speak up more easily?"

"Yes and also, studies have shown that being sexually abused puts you at a much higher risk of being assaulted again in future."

Kebi suddenly had a moment of realisation.

"That actually happened to me," she admitted.

"What happened to you?"

"I was sexually abused by someone else – my mom's cousin."

Edward did not seem surprised.

"Did it happen before or after George?"

It happened while I was being abused by George. He lived in the same neighbourhood as us and we called him Uncle Charles. He was funny and kind and I liked him because he was very attentive (to children) and always seemed genuinely interested to know what was going on in our lives. When I was ten and started looking into potential secondary schools to apply to, he made himself more available and gave me a lot of advice on choosing the right schools. As a result, he visited our home more frequently and whenever he did, he gifted the kids with pocket money. Once when he was visiting, he ran out of money and I was the only one whom he had not given money to. He felt bad although it did not matter to me.

I said, 'Uncle, it's alright; I don't really have anything to buy.'

He laughed.

'That's why I like you, Kebi,' he said, 'You are not materialistic like the others but I want to be fair to all of you so I will be expecting you in my office tomorrow to collect your own share.'

The following day, I asked my cousin, Andrew, who was twelve years old, to accompany me to Uncle Charles' office which was a twenty-minute walk from our house. When we got there he was happy to see us, as usual, but asked Andrew to come in first since he was 'older'. Uncle Charles explained that Andrew and I were nearly adults and needed privacy so he would see us one-by-one. I liked the idea of being perceived as *nearly-an-adult* and as I sat in his waiting room, I imagined being able to someday soon, stand up to George as an adult. Moments later, they emerged from his office with Uncle Charles laughing out loud while addressing Andrew.

'You have girlfriends and can't even remember their names... you better treat them well,' he chuckled, 'Otherwise I will not give you any more money.'

I wondered what girlfriends he was referring to.

'Kebi, you're next! Come in and tell me what has been going on!' he said with glee.

I went in and sat in the seat across from his desk as he closed the door.

'Don't sit so far away over there,' he said, 'A beautiful princess like you should sit in a befitting seat.'

He took my hand and led me around to *his* seat but sat down first then sat me on his laps with my back against his chest. I smiled sheepishly because it felt a bit odd since I was a *big girl and did not need to sit on my uncle's laps*. He was normally touchy-feely so it was not unusual when he started to rub his hands up and down my legs as he spoke.

'So have you narrowed down the list of schools you want to apply to?' he asked.

'Papa said...'

'No, not Papa said. Based on your own research, which schools do you want to apply to? You are growing into an independent young woman and college is just around the corner. As I have already told you, you have to start thinking for yourself.'

He put his arms around me and hugged me.

'So which is your top school?'

'Our Lady of Lourdes.'

'Is this *your* first choice or Papa's first choice?'

I hesitated and chose my words carefully.

'Papa talked about it being a really good school so I think I would like to go there.'

He tapped his feet as though he was thinking about what I had just said and my immediate reaction was to jump up since it was uncomfortable. He pulled me back and held me down and spoke cheerily.

'Sit down, let's finish talking.'

'Okay,' I said unsuspectingly.

He continued.

'So... Our Lady of Lourdes... Mm... yeah, that's a good choice... it's just that, it is all the way in Bamenda which is at least six hours away. Have you considered Saker Baptist College? It's only an hour away.'

He continued to tap his feet and hold onto me as he spoke and I really wanted to sit on a different seat since his laps were too bouncy and it was uncomfortable sitting on him. I pretended to nearly fall off but he caught me and laughed out loud.

'You are falling off when we are on land. What would you do if you were at sea?'

I smiled along although I did get the joke. Once again, I attempted to get up but he casually held me down and continued to wiggle his legs. It seemed he was knowingly holding me down but pretending not to be aware as he carried on with the conversation.

I finally spoke up.

'Uncle, I want to sit on the other chair.'

He held me even tighter and leaned further into my back.

'Ah-ah! Are you afraid of your uncle?' he said.

He seemed offended.

'Where are you hurrying to? You can stay seated here; I am not going to eat you up.'

He laughed out loud again and continued to wiggle his legs. Although it was weird, I felt compelled to remain seated. He went on to ask more questions whilst still holding me down and a couple of times while laughing, he tightened his embrace on me. I did not want to appear silly by trying to get up again so I remained in his laps for the entire visit.

He eventually let go of me and dashed into the toilet saying he needed to wash his hands; when he came back out, he thanked me for coming to see him and gave me some money. Before Andrew and I left his office, he made us promise to return the following week. I agreed to but did not go back.

The following week when he came over to our house, I was in my parents' bedroom writing when I overheard him outside asking my cousins where I was. Although I was not sure why I did not feel comfortable going out to see him, I remained in my parents' bedroom with the door locked, the entire time he visited.

The next time he came over, I hid away again but this time I heard him walk from room to room calling out to me. I heard him approach the bathroom in which I was hiding so I escaped through a side door and made my way to my parents' bedroom where I stayed for the remainder of his visit. He seemed to eventually give up his search and left. I kept this up each time he came to visit until one day, I walked into the living room and there he was, seated, talking to my dad. I had no idea he had come over but hid my surprise, greeted him and was about to walk on when he got up and exclaimed.

'Kebi, is this the cold greeting I get when I have not seen you in such a long time?'

I pursed my lips and smiled.

'Come here! Come and give me a good hug!'

He hugged me as tightly as always and in that moment, I felt guilty for hiding away from him. *He was simply an affectionate person and I should not have felt uncomfortable with how he behaved in his office that day; after all, here he was, hugging me in the same touchy-feely manner in front of my dad.*

When he broke away from the hug, he sat me on his lap and gently rubbed up and down my arm as he spoke.

'Kebi I am not happy with you because you never come to visit me in my office anymore. Everyone else comes except you, why?'

I said nothing and my dad interjected.

'You should go and see him... he is your uncle. If I die today, he is the only one who will look after all of you children.'

I smiled apologetically as my dad continued.

'Tomorrow, make sure you go and see him, okay?'

'Yes, Papa.'

As I walked away, I overheard my dad say I *seemed to have become a recluse* and Uncle Charles agreed. I went and looked up the word 'recluse' in the dictionary and felt even worse for having hidden away from him. The following day as promised, I went to his office and his secretary went in to tell him I had arrived. When she disappeared through the doors, my heart suddenly began to race and I felt nervous *for no reason*. Within moments, he came out and led me into his office, and I was relieved when he did not ask me to switch seats again.

He asked to know what I had been doing all day then offered me a soft drink which I declined after which he helped himself to one. Then out of nowhere, he came up from behind me and casually put his hand over my shoulder down into the front of my dress; I was stunned but remained still. He continued to talk as though nothing was happening; he moved his hand down to my groin as he leaned into me. I remained still but was so shocked that I began to hyperventilate; I now know that I was having a panic attack but at the time, having no understanding of what was happening was terrifying.

He withdrew his hand from inside my dress and asked what the matter was but I could not get any words out as tears streamed down my face. He wiped my eyes and continued to talk as he lifted me up and sat me on his laps, with my back against his chest like before. Then he began to wiggle his legs and bounce me on them, while touching my crotch over my underwear from time to time. I remember him saying *you can't be scared of your uncle. There's nothing to be scared of, stop crying.*

I dissociated mentally and when I came to, there was wetness on the back of my dress and I jumped up thinking I had urinated on myself; he got up quickly and said not to worry for it was just water. When he opened a side cupboard to get me a towel, I instinctively touched the back of my dress then put my hand to my nose and realised it smelled like George's semen. Just then, it dawned on me that somehow he had done what George did to me; and with that sudden realisation, I began to shiver uncontrollably. He looked terrified as he unsteadily sat me on a couch telling me everything would be okay. I tried to reassure him that I was fine but no words came out; he fanned me with a pamphlet while he anxiously asked what was happening and why I was not talking. After what seemed like ages, my shivering died down and I stood up to leave but he insisted on taking me home; on our way, he shoved some cash into my hand and told me to use it to buy myself *something nice*. I was disgusted that he was trying to buy my silence so I slipped the money underneath the passenger seat of his car.

As soon as I got home, I went to the bathroom and washed my dress with soap in a bucket of water but it still smelled of his semen. I scrubbed it with a brush but the smell was still there. I went down on all fours; I scrubbed it and I cried but in the end I put the dress in the bin because I could not get rid of the smell. I hated him for what he had done and never went to his office again but that experience taught me from a young age to always follow my intuition and since then, I always have.

After a long pause, Edward said, "Did you ever see him again?"

"Yes, he continued to visit but I ensured I was never alone with him and tried to avoid any prolonged physical contact. But despite this, he still managed to molest me one more time at his house. How this happened was, my dad sent me there early one Sunday morning to tell him to pick us up on his way to church. The thought of seeing him one-to-one was nerve-wracking but I had no choice but to go to him; when I got to his house, the gate was unlocked so I went to the back porch where I found his nephew (who was a few years older than me). I tried to get him to pass on the message to Uncle Charles but he said it would be preferable if I went to Uncle Charles' room myself to give him the message since he had said he did not want to be disturbed because his newborn baby had kept him and his wife up all night. Knowing his wife was there to serve as a buffer gave me a little comfort as I tiptoed down the corridor and knocked at their bedroom door gently.

'Who is it?' he said.

'Good morning uncle, it's Kebi. Papa says you should stop by and pick us up on your way to church because he won't be able to take us today.'

'Wait, I'm coming out.'

I certainly did not want him to come out to me so I quickly repeated what I had said and turned to leave when he came out of the room with a finger on his lips.

'The baby is sleeping,' he whispered.

158

'Sorry to disturb you uncle, Papa says you should stop by the house later and take us to church.'

He nodded and as he turned around quietly to close the door behind him, I started heading back down the corridor quickly. I had only taken a few steps when he caught up with me and in one swift motion, he pulled me backwards and pinned me up against the wall. He leaned his entire weight against me as I struggled to wriggle my miniscule ten year-old frame from beneath him.

'Please Uncle, I want to go and get ready for church,' I pleaded.

He ignored my pleas and continued to press himself against me and moan sexually. I managed to tilt my head up and look at him.

'Uncle, please I want to go home.'

He continued moaning and pressing up on me and I started to cry. Suddenly, he put his hand over my neck and viciously stuck his tongue into my mouth and moved it all around. I struggled to free myself but he tightened his grip around my neck, choking me. I bit his tongue as hard as I could and he released his grip then I escaped – he called out to me to stop but I continued running. I did not go straight home because I knew my eyes would be red from crying and I wanted the redness to subside before I went home. I went to an uncompleted building close by, stayed there for some time and went home later. I did not go to church that day and tried to avoid being alone with him from that day on.

Did He Rape You?

AT HER NINTH SESSION, Kebi continued to recount how her ordeal ended.

"Sundays in our house were quiet. I am not sure if it was simply the temperament of the day or if the noise was kept to a minimum because my dad was in bed for most of the day. One such afternoon, I joined my mom in the living room as she watched a movie on videocassette. There was a kissing scene which I felt especially uncomfortable watching due to my experiences with George and Uncle Charles. I peeked at my mom and was surprised at her nonchalance as she watched it. Just then, my dad called for her and when she left me in the living room, the kissing turned into a sex scene. That was my first realisation that this was something people actually did. My heart raced as I watched it because I knew I should not be; but what was baffling was that the woman appeared pleased rather than in pain. In the next scene, while talking to a friend, she said she had *made love* the night before. I instantly remembered seeing the words *make love* in my mom's *Woman's Own* magazines and was eager to find out more.

The following day when my parents were out, I told George I was going to clean my mom's bathroom - she had hundreds of magazines stacked in a corner in her bathroom. I locked myself in there and flipped through them. This was how I learned that making love was a good thing and that it was also called sex. Although it was confusing, what made me even more rattled was learning that sex made you pregnant.

That night, I wrote about the symptoms I had been having: tiredness, sleepiness, nausea and spotting on my underwear (as described in the magazine). I was so worried about my dad's reaction to me being pregnant that I could not sleep - I knew he would be disappointed in me and that made me sad. Even more nerve-wracking was the fact that I thought because I had been raped so many times, there were many babies in my stomach.

That night when George came to me, I told him I was pregnant and although it was pitch black in the room, I could tell he was worried.

'Who told you you are pregnant?'

'I saw it in Mama's magazine?'

'Which magazine?'

'It's called *Woman's Own* magazine.'

He paused and appeared to think about it.

'So how do you know from the magazine that you are pregnant?'

'The magazine tells you the symptoms of pregnancy and I have all the symptoms.'

He paused again.

'Are you seeing your menses?'

'My what?'

'Menses.'

I still did not know what it was.

'Have you ever seen blood on your pant?' he added.

'Sometimes.'

'Why did you not tell me?' he lashed out.

I was confused because he *did* know I bled when he raped me. I lay quietly on the floor as he continued to reproach me for not telling him I had started having periods.

'Get up and go to bed,' he said suddenly.

And he left the room without molesting me.

The following day, he asked if I had told my mom I was pregnant. When I said I had not, he warned me not to mention his name otherwise he would kill me and my brothers and decapitate us.

From that day on, there was no further penetration - he went back to using my thighs to ejaculate. At the time, my understanding was, he did not want to add to the number of babies I already had in my stomach. But sadly, that did not get rid of my problem; day and night, I worried about being pregnant. I stood sideways in front of my mom's bathroom mirror to examine my stomach since I had read that it would get bigger.

As weeks went by, my stomach remained flat. I once again referred to the magazine which explained that the stomach did not always get enlarged during the first trimester of pregnancy (which lasted three months). In three months' time, I was going to turn eleven. I thought that as soon as I did, my stomach would suddenly become enlarged overnight (since I would be in the second trimester). I was relieved to wake up with a flat stomach on my eleventh birthday.

I was eleven and a half when I received an offer of a place at my first choice of secondary school – although it was a six-hour drive from where we lived, I was eager to go there because my older brother, Ako, who was twelve, attended boarding school in the same town. He had just completed his second year at secondary school and was home for the long holidays which I was especially happy about because we were close and enjoyed playing together. Being a tomboy, I was very much myself when he was around – he taught me *pretend* karate moves and we walked around the house wearing karate head wraps and carrying sticks ready to 'defend ourselves from our attackers'; we jumped off walls and trees and even had makeshift military-based training at home. Whenever he was around, I literally followed him around mimicking *everything* he did – I even learned to walk like him and grab my crotch. Ebot and Junior usually tagged along and it was a lot of fun.

When Ako was home, George found it challenging to get me on my own since Ako and I followed one another around the house all day. I noticed that George monitored Ako's movements closely in order to seize any opportunity to have sex with me, which was usually when Ako was having a shower. Knowing this, I usually hid in a closet until Ako finished his shower but a couple of times, George found me hiding and raped me.

One day, my brothers and I were hanging out in our room when George called out to us to come and eat. As usual, Ebot, Junior and I instantly dropped what we were doing and ran out to him; we got our food and sat to eat at the dining table. Moments later, Ako joined us at the table a bit annoyed.

'Why do you guys run to George so fast whenever he calls for you?'

We said nothing and he carried on.

'It's almost as if you guys are scared of him, I don't get it.'

We continued to eat in silence but for the first time ever, I seriously considered confiding in Ako. Although he was only twelve, he was strong-willed and fearless – even my parents were wary of him because he did not tolerate nonsense from them or anyone else and did not shy away from confrontation. I knew he would cause a scene if I told him what had been happening; on the other hand, I was certain he would do everything in his power to make sure George was sent away. *But what if he was not sent away; what would happen to Ebot and Junior?*

It was a scary decision to make but that evening, Ako and I were in our room building a toy car out of scrunched up paper when I decided to go for it.

I blurted out, 'The reason why we run to George when he calls for us is because if we don't, he will beats us.'

Ako looked shocked and my heart began to race. I explained that George had maltreated us for years and Ako asked why I had not told anyone. I told him our parents were aware but that the beatings had worsened each time I told them about our maltreatment. I could see anger welling up in him and because I knew I would get into trouble for being pregnant, I did not mention George having sex with me.

Ako said, 'There was a time when Mama mentioned that you had bruises on your back; did he cause them?'

I nodded.

Holding a stick in each hand, Ako stormed out of the room.

'That guy needs to be taught a lesson,' he warned.

I suddenly felt queasy and dashed into the bathroom to relieve myself but was unable to vomit. By the time I got to the front yard, everyone was talking about the beatings and it all felt like déjà-vu as they exclaimed and asked me a million questions.

'So this boy continued beating you guys and you did not say anything, Kebi?'

'It was Papa who told him to beat us,' I retorted.

'So if Papa tells somebody to cut off head, you will sit down quietly and let them cut it?'

'I was scared...'

'Scared of what... is he God?'

Once again, no one seemed willing to understand what hell it had been for me. As I stood quietly in the midst of the chaos, tongues spewed blame at me for keeping quiet, for allowing my brothers to suffer, for telling them not to tell anyone. Someone even said it served me right because that was what happened to quiet children. A few of them admonished others for blaming me and explained that it was easy for adults to scare children into keeping quiet.

I fought back tears as they argued heatedly – I felt so guilty. Not long after, my mom returned from work and I spotted Ako vehemently confronting her as she walked in through the gate – he asked why she and my dad had allowed George to continue working for us after they were made aware that had beaten us. She dropped her bag and began to cry but this time it felt as if she cried more painfully. She went in and called my dad who was still at work.

I heard her on the phone screaming.

'Come and see what you have done to my children! Come and see what you have done!'

As for George, he was out on an errand (just like the last time) and everyone waited impatiently for his return.

I told Ako I needed the toilet just so I could get away for a moment. I went to my mom's bathroom and wailed as they continued shouting outside. I felt terrible for causing the drama and I wished I could disappear. Suddenly, I heard someone at the bathroom door and stopped to listen.

'Kebi, are you in there?'

It was my mom.

'Yes, Mama.'

'Finish and come… I want to ask you something.'

'Okay, Mama.'

When I went into her room, she tapped the bed gently and asked me to sit next to her. She looked completely drained and I noticed her hands were shaking.

'So George continued beating you people after the last time…'

'Yes, Mama.'

After a long pause, she said, 'Why did you not tell anybody?'

'Because it was Papa who told him to continue beating us.'

After another very long pause she said calmly, 'You should have told me… you shouldn't have kept quiet.'

I said, 'The last time I told you and Papa, you did not send him away so I thought if I told you again, he would still not be sent away.'

Tears streamed down her face.

'You should have told me, Kebi,' she said calmly, 'You should have told me.'

She sobbed uncontrollably while I remained silent. This was one of the things I had always dreaded; I did not want her to find out about what George had been doing to us because I wanted to protect her from the pain of blaming herself. Tears ran down my cheeks as I watched her cry then suddenly she took a deep breath and dried her eyes. For the first time that day, she looked at me.

'I want to ask you something,' she said.

I looked at her and waited... and kept waiting.

'Did he rape you?' she said finally.

I didn't know what rape meant.

'Did he what?'

'I said did he rape you?' she said a little louder.

'I don't know what...'

She grabbed my shoulders and started shaking me and shouting.

'Did he rape you! Please tell me, Kebi! Did he rape you?'

She seemed desolate but I didn't know what rape meant and before I knew it, she was on the floor lamenting.

'This boy has killed me! He has killed me! Kebi did he rape you? Please tell me!'

I burst into tears and cried out.

'I don't know!'

Before I knew it, I was next to her on the floor crying.

Moments later, there was a commotion outside; it sounded like George had returned and was pounced on by the mob. My mom raced out but I stayed in her room from where I listened to the chaos; I could tell that some neighbours had joined in and within minutes, the clamour had become so loud that I literally could not make out what was being said anymore. I finally came out when my dad's car pulled up. The scene in the yard was horrific; George was lying on the concrete floor with blood trickling from all over his body. His hands were tied in front of him with a thick rope and he was quiet as they hurled insults at him. I could tell my dad had been crying; he immediately asked everyone to gather in the living room and asked my

172

uncles to bring George in after everyone had gone in. Once we settled into the living room, we heard scuffling and shouting as George was viciously kicked and shoved in; he was pushed to the floor when they entered the living room. His face was unrecognisable underneath multiple grooves of blood and dangling, discoloured skin. He promptly began to cry and beg for forgiveness but my uncles and older cousins scolded him ruthlessly as my mom wept in a corner.

Desperately fighting back tears, my dad asked me and Ebot to go and bring everything George had ever used to beat us and as we headed to the kitchen, we hugged each other excitedly.

'They are going to send him away this time,' I beamed.

We took frying pans, lids of pots, pestles, grinding stones, wooden utensils and metallic cooking spoons; then we went to George's room and returned with belts, cables and large tree branches which he kept under his bed. We placed them on the floor next to him and everyone gasped in shock. One of my uncles immediately grabbed hold of a pestle and another drew out a cutlass and they both lunged at George and beat him mercilessly.

'How can a grown man use such things to beat little children?' they shouted.

While they beat him up, my dad motioned for me to take my siblings away and as we left, the noise grew exponentially. From our bedroom, we listened to the commotion as he was viciously battered. His screams were absolutely terrifying and as I heard him plead for his life, I recalled how much I had begged him over the years to stop beating us.

Much later, three police officers came over to take him away and there was one last scuffle as he resisted being arrested but they finally managed to handcuff him. We followed them outside and watched him being bundled into the back of the police car. My eyes were fixated on him – I enjoyed seeing him in pain. Suddenly our eyes met and he smiled eerily but I continued to glare at him. In that moment it dawned on me that I was not scared of him anymore.

Post-traumatic Stress Disorder

AS KEBI STRUTTED into the tenth session, she spoke with a sense of urgency.

"At last week's session I forgot to mention that I turned out not pregnant after all."

"Well, that's a relief... how did you find this out?"

"I just waited and waited and nothing happened so I assumed I was never pregnant to begin with."

"Did you mention it to anyone after that?"

She shook her head.

"Did your mom bring it up?"

"No one did," she smiled, "from the minute George left until I left for college, it was as if he never existed. No one spoke about him - at least not to me - and no further questions were asked about what happened. He was no longer *with* us but no one knew he was still very present in my head. I kept seeing him wherever I went but when I turned to look, he was not there. I felt his eyes on me *constantly*... and I soon became a walking bundle of nerves. Whenever I managed to fall asleep at night, I had recurring dreams in which I was raped and tortured and woke up several times petrified that he had returned. Unfortunately, there was no one to talk to about this so I carried on as normal during the day and that became my norm. At night it was more difficult and I cried myself to sleep a lot. I continued to document my feelings but every day was a struggle and somehow I learnt how to compartmentalize and dispel painful thoughts when they arose."

Edward chimed in.

"I am pleasantly surprised that you have made it this far in your life with no formal therapy."

Kebi nodded.

"It hasn't been easy."

After a while, Edward said, "Have you heard anything about George since?"

She took a deep breath.

"After he was taken away, one day my mom sent me to a nearby store to buy something; I was on my way back home when I looked up and saw someone who

176

looked like George. But given that I had *seen* him on many occasions and it turned out never to be him, I did not think it was. As he got closer, I saw that it was him. I tried to run past but he grabbed my arm and cupped my cheeks tightly.

He said, 'Did I not tell you I will come back and deal with you?'

I could not believe it was actually him. He suddenly looked up past me and I ducked and ran off. I told my dad about what happened and we later found out he had been released from police custody and was living somewhere in our neighbourhood. My dad asked for further enquiries to be made to determine where he lived but no further information was available. From then on, I really started living in fear; I checked the gates at our house multiple times a day to ensure it was locked; I was frightened to go to the toilet at night and never left home unaccompanied. Even so, I never spoke to anyone about the psychological torture I was going through and at that juncture I could not wait to go to boarding school where he would not find me since it was in a different town.

On my last night at home before I left for boarding school, I took one last walk through the entire house. I went from room to room and bathroom to bathroom and it was like walking through multiple dungeons of savage pain. Harrowing memories rushed forth with a force so cosmic that when I got to the *brown toilet*, somehow I was knocked to the ground. And only in that moment did I truly *feel* the monstrousness of what we had endured.

After a long pause, Edward said, "Have you ever gone back to the house?"

"I have, it is our family home... I was at boarding school for seven years and at the end of every school term, I went back there and even slept in the same room on same bed. But as years went by, I felt less distressed being there. I was even able to use the *brown toilet* without experiencing any painful memories whatsoever... they just sort of disappeared."

Edward smiled subtly.

He explained.

"There is a form of psychotherapy known as Prolonged Exposure Therapy which is used to treat Post-Traumatic Stress Disorder (PTSD). When you initially felt distressed while going from room to room in your house, that was a classic sign of PTSD. But by repeatedly going back to the scene of the trauma (the rooms in your house), you gradually became desensitized and this ultimately allowed you not to feel distressed whilst there."

Kebi jotted in amazement.

"I hated going home at the end of every school term. It never crossed my mind that going home was essentially helping me heal."

Edward smiled proudly.

"And this applies to any form of trauma; repeated exposure to traumatic memories, things or places enables you to feel less and less distressed every time you are exposed to them and can lead to a full recovery in the end."

Pensively, she said, "I won't say I have made a full recovery but I definitely have no problems being in any room in our house. This is not to say I have completely forgotten about things that happened there; I just don't feel the pain from the memories anymore unless I allow myself to really think about them in detail."

Edward nodded.

179

"You mentioned looking forward to going to boarding school; while there, did you have any problems due to your abuse?"

She paused momentarily.

"I would say the main issue was my lack of focus; memories popped into my head willy-nilly and although I often managed to dispel them momentarily, it rendered me distracted. It was better during the day since there were ongoing school activities to partake in and also, I loved being around my friends because we had so much fun that I did not have time to stop and think about my past as frequently. But as soon as the lights went out at night, I was left all alone with my painful memories. It was nearly impossible to sleep and when I finally fell asleep, I woke up from recurring nightmares at least once a night."

"Did you speak to anyone in school about it... a teacher maybe...?"

"I did, actually... there was a priest I spoke to once during confession. I blamed myself for everything that happened so I felt the need to confess my sin. He was the first person I ever told I was raped so I was an emotional wreck while talking to him; but after confessing to him, he took me to the side to console me since I was weeping and shaking."

"Did you find it helpful speaking to him?"

"Tremendously... he suggested I talk to my family and friends about it so they would better support me. I remember that at some point whilst talking to him, he held my hands and I noticed he was trying not to cry; he said, 'My daughter, I am so sorry you went through something so horrible but you have to know that it was *not* your fault. It was *not* your fault.' He continued to repeat that it was not my fault and the more he said it, the more I cried because he did not even know me but he believed me."

Kebi dried her eyes and saw that Edward was dabbing his too.

She said, "I'm sorry, I cry every time I think about those words – It Was Not Your Fault."

"They were certainly words you needed to hear," said Edward.

She nodded.

"Those five words are words that anyone who has ever been raped will definitely benefit from hearing; for me, it was profoundly therapeutic for the priest to say them to me. It helped to strip away the guilt and self-blame I had been living with for years."

There was a long pause then Edward sighed and switched gears.

"You mentioned your friends earlier... you said you loved being around them."

Kebi smiled.

"I did... we laughed a lot. For some reason, we were always laughing; it seemed as if because we laughed at the silliest things, it made other situations also seem funny so we laughed endlessly... I loved those times."

"So they were close friends..."

"For sure."

"Were they aware of your abuse?"

"I told some of them but not in detail... I think I told two or three of them that I was raped but that was it. The person to whom I gave a little more information was my very first boyfriend, John, whom I started dating at the age of thirteen. The first couple of times he tried to kiss me, I experienced flashbacks of being forced to suck George's tongue, so I felt the need to explain why I reacted oddly."

Edward nodded, "How did he take it when you told him you were abused?"

"Very well, actually – he was only three years older than me but quite mature and when he found out about my abuse, he was extremely compassionate. But the effects of the abuse were still very raw for me at the time. For example, a couple of times, John mentioned he found it difficult to hold a conversation with me because I seemed disengaged. I knew exactly what he meant because most of the time (in life in general), I felt completely disengaged from life."

"Would you kindly elaborate on that?" Edward said.

"Sure. It was challenging for me to be fully present and engage in a conversation without being mentally pulled away by a painful memory. There were many things that triggered such memories: smells, sounds, songs playing on the radio, crickets chirping, children crying, someone pronouncing words like George, smiling like him, chewing like him and even seeing boiled rice. But the thing that rattled me the most was physical contact and although John and I did not have sex in the four years we dated, it was really difficult for me being in the relationship because every touch reminded me of George."

Edward sighed.

"I applaud you for being able to recognize aspects that you found challenging to deal with after your abuse. It shows that you had gradually begun to heal, whether you knew it or not. During the time when you were with your boyfriend, John, you seemed to have developed a relatively clear perspective..."

"Sorry to interrupt you, Edward..."

"It's okay..."

"Erm, I don't think I had anything close to a clear perspective as you were trying to say. John and I stopped dating when I was seventeen and I travelled to England for university at eighteen. Three months after coming to England, I was physically assaulted by a family friend who tried to forcefully have sex with me and guess what, just like before, I didn't tell anyone about it," she shrugged her shoulders disappointedly.

"I am sorry to hear that."

Kebi sighed.

"If I had any clarity in my perspective, at the age of eighteen I ought to have learned from the past and known that I should report the asshole to the police for trying to force himself on me, but I did not."

"Why did you not?" Edward said calmly.

Kebi shook her head.

"I did not want to cause any trouble since he was a family friend. I first met him at eighteen but he was already known to the family. After a couple of weeks of meeting him, he asked me to be his girlfriend and I said no then he offered to show me around my new town since I was new in England and did not have any friends yet. Desperate for a new chapter in my life, I was thrilled at the prospect of trying new things and meeting new people so he and I started hanging out every weekend."

"How old was he?"

"Twenty-seven."

"Okay."

Kebi sighed.

"He was loud, fun to be around and always had at least two women with him whenever he came to pick me up for a night out. However, one night, he took me out on my own to make up for missing my nineteenth birthday and that night he asked me, once again, to be his girlfriend. I smiled and said nothing - I was still very reserved at the time and did not talk much. I guess because I did not say anything, he began to ask about my sexual activity.

'So are you a virgin?' he said.

'Not really.'

'So you're sexually active?'

I shook my head.

'No.'

'When was the last time you had sex then?'

'I've never really had sex.'

He laughed and looked at me like *you poor thing*. Then he said, 'Tell me, what does you've never really had sex mean? You've either had it or you haven't; you're not a virgin so you *must* have had sex, it can't really be in between, can it?'

I felt comfortable with him so I explained that I had been raped and that since then I had not had sex.

With a look of great resolve, he took a long sip of his beer.

He said, 'If you agree to be my woman, believe me, I will fuck you so hard and so good that your brain will forget that you were ever raped.'

I did not expect such a response and for some reason it really hurt my feelings but I said nothing.

He said, 'What are you looking at me like that for, I'm fucking amazing at that shit, mate, trust me.'

I looked at the time and told him I was ready to go home but he did not want me to.

'You ain't got no lectures tomorrow; let's go to my place instead.'

I lived with relatives in a family house so I used that as my excuse.

'My family will not be happy to hear that I went home with you, Fabien.'

'Why are you always worrying about what your fucking family thinks? You're a grown ass woman, stop worrying about them; we're in England mate!'

I feigned a smile.

'I think you have had too much beer. Please take me home.'

On the car ride home, he reiterated that I was an adult and needed to make my own decisions about whom I wanted to date and what I wanted to do and to stop thinking about what my family would say. The more he dwelled it, the more I saw reason with him and suddenly found him more appealing. When we parked outside my place, we stayed in the car for a few minutes as I listened to him profess his admiration for me then he leaned in for a kiss. Feeling very much like the renegade he wished I was, I indulged in the kiss then felt his hand on my thigh which resulted in an uppercut to his chin.

'What the fuck!' he shouted.

'I'm sorry I didn't mean to hit you...'

He looked bewildered and I felt terrible.

'What the fuck was that about?' he shouted.

'I don't know how to explain it... my body sometimes reacts like that when it feels weird.'

'But how did it feel weird, it's just a fucking kiss.'

'I know but because of my past, I think I need time to get used to this type of stuff. Some parts of my body spark bad memories and reactions that I can't control, I am really sorry.'

Given the manner in which he stared at me, I could tell he had never seen any such thing before then he smiled and shook his head.

'I have told you to come spend the night with me and I will fuck away those fucking memories babe, they will become history, trust me.'

I tried to smile although I was still trying to recover from the flashback.

'Come on, give us a smile,' he said.

I forced a smile and in that moment as I looked at him, I knew I was never going to be his girlfriend and I knew I was not going to have sex with him. But what I was most certain about was that it would be a very long time before I had sex with anyone.

He came over a week later, on Millennium Eve and the first thing he said was he knew I was home alone and came to ring in the New Year with me. My relatives had told him they would be away for a few days and that it would be nice if he could come over to check on me.

As soon as we sat down to watch the New Year's festivities on TV, my phone rang and it was a call from a family member overseas wishing me a Happy New

189

year. I was on the phone for nearly forty minutes and seated on a separate sofa from him. Although he was watching TV, I caught him sneak a peek at my legs - I was wearing a knee-length satin nightdress with a matching robe over it so I pulled the robe over my knees and continued the phone call.

Moments later, I noticed him glance at my legs again. In high school, I was insecure about my legs because a boy in my class repeatedly cracked jokes about them and said they were masculine. So, I became self-conscious when Fabien repeatedly looked at them and I went upstairs and wore oversized cotton pyjama trousers underneath my nightdress and came back downstairs. Several minutes later, I finished the call and Fabien said he wanted to ask me something.

'What the fuck did you go wear those ugly trousers for?'

Not one to say much, I smiled and rolled my eyes playfully.

'Leave my trousers alone; I like them.'

I crossed my legs and changed the topic because he liked to dwell on insignificant things.

'It looks like you've been out already... I can tell you have had a few drinks,' I smiled.

'Why are you trying to change the topic?'

I never took most of what he said seriously especially when he had been drinking.

'Change what topic?' I said.

'These fucking ugly trousers... look at them.'

He leaned over to touch them but I moved my legs away, shook my head and continued flipping through channels.

'Are you ignoring me?' he asked.

Without taking my eyes off the TV, I said, 'Fabien, I am not ignoring you. I don't know what you want me to say... are we seriously talking about my pyjamas right now?'

'Of course, we're talking about your fucking pyjamas... what else do you think we're talking about?'

He was the most dramatic person I had ever met.

Edward asked, "In that moment, did you feel intimidated?"

"Of course not, I had no reason to feel intimidated or scared because it was Fabien. He talked a lot more whenever he had had alcohol so to me this was normal behaviour from him. At some point, he came over to me and tugged at my robe and said, 'Why are you not saying anything?'

Nonchalantly, I pulled my robe back.

I said, 'Fabien, what is it with my pyjamas? I thought you came over to hang out.'

He tugged at my robe again and raised his voice.

'I asked you a fucking question and you're telling me bullshit. Answer the fucking question!'

I sat up as I responded.

'What are you shouting about? You're taking this joke too far, Fabien, sit down and let's just watch TV.'

Stubbornly, he tugged at my robe again; I pulled it back and he tugged at it again.

I started getting irritated.

'Fabien, what is your actual problem, please leave my clothes alone.'

'What's my problem? What the fuck is *your* problem?'

He pulled my robe so hard, it ripped at the seam near my arm and I got up, startled.

'Fabien, what is this? You've torn my robe, it's not funny.'

192

I then expected him to break out of character and apologize but instead he pushed me back down onto the sofa in anger – that was when I realised he was serious.

'Sit your ass down!' he said, 'You went upstairs to wear ugly fucking trousers and you can't tell me why! What did you think I was gonna do, rape you?'

I did not see that coming and he still had a firm grip on my robe as I disputed what he had said. I pulled away as we barked at each other and my robe continued to rip. There was a scuffle and before I knew it, I was backing up into the kitchen with a knife in my hand.

'Fabien, if you don't leave right now, I swear I will stab you... please don't make me do it.'

He had an evil look in his eye that I had never seen before. He smiled then dropped his gaze to my chest and that brought back the memory of George staring at my naked body in the *brown toilet*. With the realisation that Fabien was going to try to have sex with me, I tightened my grip on the knife as he continued staring at my chest. In that instant, I decided I *would* push the knife into his stomach if he lunged at me and suddenly he did. I rushed forward with the knife and he quickly sprang back and stopped; he looked stunned.

'You were actually going to fucking stab me!'

'Fabien, you know I really don't want to do this so please just leave.'

Before I knew it, he hit my hand and the knife fell down.

'I'm begging, please leave me alone!' I implored.

He slapped me across the face and shouted. 'What's wrong with you... why are you fucking yelling... you want the neighbours to come over? I can't believe you were going to fucking stab me! For what? For fucking what?'

I tried to run past him out of the kitchen but he grabbed hold of my trousers and I kneed him in the penis shouting at him to leave me alone. He screamed and let go of me. I dashed out and headed up the stairs where he caught up with me and dragged me down viciously, ripping off what was left of my clothing. Then I felt a heavy thud on my right shoulder which disoriented me. As I lay on the floor, I could tell he was shouting in my face but it sounded like I was under water. He slapped me again and my vision was blurry but I was well aware that I needed to get away from him; I pushed and willed myself to get up but could not move.

I cried as I watched him continue to shout in my face and suddenly I felt a surge of energy well up inside me and I pleaded for him to leave me alone.

He pulled me up by the hand.

'Get the fuck up!' he said.

It took a little while but as soon as I got up, I scrambled up the stairs with him following closely behind. No sooner had I flung myself into my bedroom and shut the door, did he start pounding on it.

'Kebi, open the door! Open this door now!'

He tried to push it but I held it shut from inside. He slammed into it repeatedly until it broke near the top hinge, at which point I let go and jumped onto my bed. As I stood on my bed, naked, pleading with him, I wondered how this was happening again. In that moment, I knew there was nothing I could do to stop him; I accepted the fact that he was going to rape me and I cried. He looked enraged as I knelt on my bed and continued to plead.

'Fabien, I am begging you, please don't do this.'

'Don't do what! Huh? Rape you? To rape what off you? No tits, no ass! What the fuck is there to rape?'

He hit me in the left side of my face and I fell to the side. I felt faint as he turned me over onto my back and placed his knees on both my arms then began to undo his belt.

I did not fight back. But when I caught sight of his penis, I recalled George raping me and suddenly became determined not to let it happen again. I amassed all the strength I had and began to wiggle nonstop. He asked me to stop moving about and when I did not, he hit me and I drew my arm from underneath his knee and punched him in the eye as hard as I could. He tried to reposition his knees to pin me down again but I wiggled all the more as he continued to shout.

'Stop being so fucking difficult!'

I caught sight of my closet right next to my bed; it always wobbled because one leg at the front was shorter than the three others. I placed my foot on my closet and pushed on it and it toppled and fell on us with a loud bang. He was confused about what had happened and let go of me although he was still on top of me. I quickly fought my way out from underneath him, scrambled over the closet (which was now on him) and I headed for the stairs.

He shouted at me to come back but I was already at the bottom of the stairs and knew I had to get out of the house but was naked. I spotted a long winter coat hung behind the door, grabbed it, opened the door and ran. I put on the coat as I ran and after a few right and left turns, I stopped to catch my breath and only then did I realise I was barefoot. It was freezing, my feet were numb and my jaws stung; I looked around and had no idea where I was.

The streets were completely bare and suddenly I heard fireworks followed by jubilation – it was midnight and people were rejoicing as they rang in the New Year 2000.

My feet were especially painful on the frosty tarmac - I saw a building with steps in front of it and ran over; I sat at the steps and got my feet off the tarmac. When I sat down, I tucked my feet into the coat. I trembled excessively since it was the middle of winter and as I looked around and saw no one, I cried. My ears were numb so I tried to cover them with the coat when I realised it had an oversized fluffy hood which I pulled over my head and doubled over to keep warm. I was slightly lightheaded so I sank my head between my thighs and fell asleep.

I thought I heard a dog whine in the distance yet at the same time it felt like it was right next to me. I was about to drift back to sleep when I heard it again and feebly opened my eyes and realised it was daylight.

I heard someone say, 'Come here!'

I opened my eyes and there was a dog seated at my feet as its owner called out to it. Although it hurt to move, I managed to tilt my head just enough to spot the person a few yards away from me. He came closer, stooped down and asked if I as okay; he was a priest. He smiled and I tried to smile back but my face would not budge; plus, it hurt as I shivered. He said he would take me inside so I could warm up. He put an arm on my back to help me up but ended up lifting me to my feet since I was frozen stiff. As he carried me in, I realised I had spent the night crouched over at the steps of a church. He took me to a back room inside the church and sat me next to a radiator which I immediately leaned against. He asked what my name was and where I lived but I could not speak. Then he went out to get someone to assist me and returned almost immediately, with two elderly women who came in smiling. They welcomed me, brought me tea and a blanket and invited me to attend the morning service with them.

I sat there for a while but was anxious at the thought of having to explain to them what had happened. I blamed myself for leading Fabien on by allowing him to kiss me that time in his car; he must have assumed I liked him and wanted to have sex. The more I thought about it, the worse I felt for having caused it; when the elderly women left to get things ready for the morning service, I left the church immediately.

Once I was outside, I remembered I had come up along the road to my right so I hurried down that road hoping no one would notice me since I was barefoot. Fortunately, there was no one in the streets, leading me to guess it was very early in the morning. Suddenly, I realised I did not have my keys and was unsure how I would get into the house. Worse still, *what if Fabien was still there?* I eventually found my way home and to my greatest surprise, the door was open and he wasn't there.

Not only was my bedroom door broken but my room was in shambles. Despite the dishevelled piles of stuff that had been emptied out of my closet onto my bed the night before, (with the winter coat still on) I squeezed my way under the covers and cried myself to sleep. For the next couple of days, I used ice packs and warm compresses and when my relatives returned, all they noticed was my broken door for which I gave an excuse. But I spoke to no one about the incident which to me, implies I was definitely not thinking clearly, although at the time I might have thought I was."

Edward explained.

"I understand. I must also mention that you did not lead Fabien on in any way. He tried to manipulate you into dating him and when that did not work he sought to have sex with you by any means necessary. Even if you were in a relationship with him, it would be criminal for him to force himself on you."

Kebi nodded.

"Of course I get that now but back then I was really naive and I also think my abuse affected me in ways I never even realised, like being unable to recognise an abusive person like him. Simply the manner in which he spoke to all the women he hung out with, including me, was not respectful but we continued to hang out with him and accept being spoken to in the manner in which he did."

Edward agreed.

"Childhood emotional wounds (especially sexual abuse) can adversely affect you but the good news is such emotional wounds do not have to be permanent. And being here addressing these issues, increasing your awareness and knowledge of them is useful for your healing. With time, you can unlearn such toxic lessons and be able to react differently in abusive situations."

Edward let her finish jotting before he continued.

"What about Fabien; did you hear from him again?"

"I did, he came over to the house a few days after the attack and acted as if nothing had happened; he even remarked that I seemed a bit quiet. At the time, I was perplexed and wondered if he truly had no recollection of what had happened but after that day, he never came back again. This implied to me he fully remembered what happened. But many years later, I heard he was in jail for domestic violence towards his girlfriend."

Intimacy

KEBI EXPERIENCED MULTIPLE flashbacks daily after recounting her attack by Fabien but with the support of her husband, Ofe, she got through them and praised his efforts at her next therapy session.

"Right from the beginning before we even started dating, he was refreshing to be around because he was funny, so it allowed me no room to think about my past. He even indirectly helped to get rid of some of my PTSD by turning it into laughter."

Edward wondered how abuse could be turned into anything funny.

"Would you mind giving me an example of this?" he smiled.

Kebi thought briefly.

"One example that springs to mind is when he found out about my phobia of masculine-smelling bathrooms."

Edward was intrigued.

"You have a phobia of male bathrooms?"

"I used to but not anymore because when he found out about it, he made a funny sexual remark which made me laugh a lot; from then on, whenever I experienced the phobia, I remembered his funny remark; and with time, the phobia disappeared."

Edward cleared his throat.

"How did this phobia of male bathrooms manifest itself?"

"Well, it was not exactly a phobia of *male* bathrooms; if *any* bathroom was last used by an adult male, I felt like I could smell their semen long after they had left the bathroom and the smell made me nauseous."

Edward nodded as she continued.

"So I was always strategic in using bathrooms; I never went in after a male."

"Did you ever go in after Ofe?"

"I tried not to but could not always avoid it; when we first started dating, whenever I spent the night at his place I woke up early to use the toilet and shower before him then I went back to sleep."

Edward seemed intrigued.

"Your bathroom phobia is a form of PTSD which (like any other) if not dealt with, can usually last for the remainder of a person's life. For some people the symptoms gradually fade over time which seems to be the case for you, otherwise there is treatment for it."

"What – like medication?"

He sighed.

"Medication can be prescribed for PTSD but not always – it depends on the individual. In the first instance, psychotherapy is used to guide you through dealing with difficult emotions and there are other useful techniques like yoga and meditation."

Kebi finished jotting.

"Well, thankfully I don't experience it anymore," she smiled gleefully.

"When did you first notice this phobia?"

"I was thirteen or fourteen when I first noticed it; I went into a public restroom one day and was floored by the stench of semen which reminded me of George. From that day on, I seemed to develop a heightened sensitivity to the smell and unfortunately attributed masculine (bathroom) smells to it."

205

"Did this pose any problems with you and Ofe in terms of intimacy?"

Kebi chuckled as she thought about all the sexual issues she had dealt with through the years.

"I *always* had problems with intimacy and because I was not accustomed to speaking up about things that bothered me, it led to bigger problems in our relationship."

"How long have you and Ofe been together, if you don't mind me asking?"

"I don't mind at all. We started dating when I was nineteen and got married when I was thirty."

"That's quite a few years," Edward gasped.

Kebi nodded smiling.

"It's gone by quite fast."

"Do you mind if we talk a bit about how things were when you and Ofe first met?"

"No, I would love to," she said pleasantly.

"How long after you met did he find out about your abuse?"

"Oh I told him within the first week of meeting him. Mind you, when we first met, I was dating someone else so he and I were just friends but had similar interests, so we ended up running into each other a lot on the university campus; we became close very fast."

"How did he react to finding out you were abused?"

Kebi thought back to that time and smiled.

"I think he received it well – he did not say much, to be honest, but I don't know whether it was because he did not know what to say or if he was just being a good listener."

Edward explained.

"It can be nerve-wracking for anyone to hear that someone they care about was raped, so I commend him for reacting sensitively towards you, whether it was intentional or not. Simply listening is enough."

"It worked for me," she smiled.

Edward went on.

"Most often, when someone has been sexually abused, people ask questions to try to understand how the abuse happened and the tendency is to question why the victim did not take preventative measures. For example, they might be questioned on why they wore revealing clothing or why they went home with a stranger. Such questions can make the victim blame themselves even more and that can be detrimental; so like I said, just listening is the best option. When you first told Ofe, did he ask any questions?"

"He mostly listened but also asked where my parents were during the abuse and why I did not tell anyone."

"How did you feel about him asking those questions?"

"It was fine - I didn't mind talking about it."

"How long after that did you start your relationship?"

"We started dating a couple of months later when my previous relationship ended."

"Did Ofe have any concerns about intimacy?"

"He asked if the abuse had made me hate sex. I definitely hated sex but told him I was fine with it because I did not want to scare him away. Also, at the time, I erroneously thought I could handle my negative feelings about sex."

"What sorts of challenges did you face?"

Kebi sighed as she recalled her struggles.

"Sorry, I might get a bit graphic..."

"That's okay, as long as *you're* comfortable talking about it."

She smiled.

"Thank you... I had many challenges when it came to intimacy. The underlying issue was I simply Hated. Being. Intimate. Just kissing, brought back memories of George sucking my tongue and that made me want to vomit. During our first ten years together, I tried tirelessly to avoid kissing Ofe; it was hard but I could not bring myself to explain (to him) why I shied away from kissing him. But thankfully, I eventually overcame it; I got to a point where I desperately wanted to be 'normal' and enjoy my relationship and my life as a whole. I learned and realised that a shift in my perspective was needed for this to happen and I began to work on it."

"What did you do to work on it?"

"I read a bit on intimacy and learned a few lessons including the fact that kissing helped people to connect romantically. I had struggled to maintain such a connection with Ofe for many years and was determined to fix it, so I literally practised with him. At first, it was awful because it tasted like George; but I endured it and repeatedly reminded myself that I was doing it with Ofe, who loved me dearly and with whom I was desperate to reconnect and bond. It was not easy but in time, that vile feeling completely vanished. It took a lot of work to change my mind set but that was how my issue with kissing was resolved."

She paused then carried on.

"In the same light, I hated all romantic physical contact, down to holding hands. I also preferred being fully-clothed during sex in order to reduce the amount of skin-to-skin contact since that reminded me of George's skin against mine. This went on for nearly eleven years and when I began to work on my issues with intimacy, I addressed it head-on. How I did this was by giving myself the difficult task of incrementally increasing the amount of skin-to-skin contact I had with Ofe each time we were intimate. I exposed a little more skin than the time before, each time we were intimate. It was nerve-wracking because my skin and my entire being were not used to such massive levels of skin contact but my determination to cut myself away from my abuse was my driving force. With time, it got better and today, that issue is non-existent."

Edward was curious.

"What was it that prompted you to do something about these issues?"

Kebi sighed.

"I had lots of friends and acquaintances whilst at university and there was a lot of talk about boys, sex and relationships. I wanted to be able to experience the nice warm feelings they spoke of in relation to their sex lives. I longed to feel what they felt when they talked about holding their partners hands, kissing and being intimate. Although I had been in relationships, I had never felt those things in all my life. There was always something in me that prevented those warm feelings from reaching deep down inside me. I didn't know what it was. But when I forced myself to change the way I viewed intimacy as a whole, my mind and body eventually followed suit."

"Did you have any problems with physical contact in a non-romantic context like hugging or shaking hands with people and so on?"

"Not at all," she chuckled, "in fact, I was a *big* hugger and still am; I even hug people who I have just met for the first time. But surprisingly, I had problems hugging my *daughter* from around the time when she started walking at twelve months old."

Edward appeared intrigued as he listened on.

"I breastfed her for about sixteen months so she was in my arms a lot; but when she began to walk, at times I felt uneasy cuddling her. It was psychologically torturous because I did not understand what the unease was about. I spoke to a midwife who explained that it was either related to postnatal depression (which I had been diagnosed with), my childhood abuse or both. She asked me to see my doctor for a referral to psychotherapy but when I went to see the doctor, I somehow forgot to mention it. I therefore ended up trying to deal with it on my own."

"How did you deal with it?"

"I just intentionally cuddled her *all the time* and told her how much I loved her. I could feel how much she loved my cuddles, so even when it felt uncomfortable for me, I hung in there and kept her in my embrace, regardless. For me, the goal was to give her what she needed. It took a few months to recover from my postnatal depression but when I did, the discomfort in cuddling her completely disappeared."

Edward explained.

"Mothers who were sexually abused as children sometimes experience more intense or prolonged postnatal depression than those who were not. That may have been what happened in your case so I am glad you were able to resolve it."

"Yeah, me too," she said as she jotted quickly. He waited for her to finish before he continued.

"I wanted to touch on what you explained so beautifully earlier. The issues you had with intimacy and feeling disconnected are classic symptoms of sexual abuse. Simply put, it stems from the fact that when you are sexually abused, the world no longer seems like a safe place, so deep down you no longer trust others. You might think you do but you really don't. In trying to reconnect with Ofe, you essentially broke down the protective walls you had built around you and you thereby became more open to pre-existing and new relationships."

Kebi nodded as she wrote down what he said.

She said, "What you just said is very accurate because when I resolved my intimacy issues (in my

213

head), I noticed that I became chattier with others, more confident and just more myself."

"More open?"

"Definitely more open... but that openness brought forth a bigger problem which I need to explain in detail, to give you the full picture. When I was raped as a child, it was too painful and traumatic to bear, so every time I was being raped, my mind mentally removed me from the situation in order for me not to feel anything. So, essentially, whenever I was being raped as a child, I was not really there (mentally or physically) and never felt anything; neither pain nor pleasure. And when the rape was over, I 'regained consciousness', then felt excruciating vaginal pain. When I became sexually active as an adult, I continued to be mentally and physically absent during sex and I had no control over it. So for eleven years, I was always completely absent during sex and did not feel a thing... but guess what... I did not know it was abnormal because that was how my body had always behaved during sexual encounters."

Edward nodded.

"That process of mentally or physically removing yourself from a situation which your body deems 'traumatic' is called dissociation."

"Yeah, I saw it online," she said lively, "I was shocked to find out there was a name for it and that many people experienced it. In *my* case, the dissociation stopped on its own after I learned to become comfortable with romantic physical contact. However, when the dissociation stopped occurring, I acquired a different problem which was a lot worse than dissociation. The problem was, because I could now feel the physicality of sexual intercourse, I felt as though I was being raped again and again every single time I had sex with Ofe."

Edward nodded sympathetically and explained.

"This is a common occurrence in survivors of sexual abuse; in *your* case, your first experience of sex was rape (and pain), so the next time you were able to *feel* sexual intercourse, it is not unusual that (to you) it feels exactly like it did the first time."

"I see... it was frustrating going through it. I did not want to hurt Ofe's feelings by telling him I felt like he was raping me; but I did not feel comfortable talking to anyone about it, so I endured it."

"That must have been difficult," said Edward.

"It was... and it hurt too but I sort of assumed that everyone felt some degree of pain during sex, which they eventually got used to then began to feel pleasure thereafter. It simply did not make sense to me especially since all my experiences with sex had only ever been painful; I actually believed women moaned because sex hurt. At some point, I spoke to Ofe about the pain and we got some creams and lubricant from the pharmacy a few times but they did not help."

"How long was it before things changed?"

She sighed.

"Things changed progressively over time... when I was twenty-five, there was a turning point one day when I was hanging out with three girlfriends and the topic of discussion soon changed to sex (as a pleasurable activity). I had previously heard people refer to it as such but never had the courage to ask why they felt that way. While hanging out with my girlfriends that afternoon, I asked how they were able to have so much sex when it was painful. They laughed and said it only hurt if it was *done roughly and for long*. When I told them my experiences had always been painful, they suggested I use lubricants, which I told them had not helped. One of them suggested I try using larger quantities of lubricant and that would help me reach orgasm faster - that was the first time I heard the word orgasm. My other girlfriend described in detail what helped her to reach orgasm, including sex positions and what not. I was completely lost. The third girl, Athena, whom I was closest to, bragged that she did not need lubricant to orgasm - she said simply wearing tight jeans *did it* for her and she suggested I try that. It was all extremely confusing to me so I jumped in at some point."

'What does orgasm mean?' I asked.

I still remember the stunned looks on their faces when I asked that but nonetheless they were more than happy to school me when they realised how ignorant I was. We talked for a further three hours during which I learnt about the workings of the female sexual anatomy including the fact that the clitoris was sensitive. Mine was not. They taught me about sensitive spots on the male and female body and made suggestions on how to determine one's sensitivities. Athena went even further to describe what an orgasm felt like and ways in which to achieve one. When I left them that evening, I was overwhelmed and excited to have learned so much and could not wait to get home to Ofe to try what I had learned.

Later that night, I was devastated when everything they suggested did not work for me. Over the next few weeks, they encouraged me to continue trying but after multiple attempts, I gave it up and accepted that there was something seriously wrong with me. But even with this crushing realisation, I still kept Ofe in the dark (about my struggles) for a further few years, until the birth of our second child when I was twenty-nine. By this time, it had been ten years since I had begun to be sexually active and experience the sexual difficulties without really talking to him about them.

After the birth of our son, I gained some weight and started jogging to get fit. While I was out jogging one evening, I experienced a sensation which felt like what Athena had previously described as an orgasm and as soon as I got home, I looked it up online and found that it was common to get an orgasm during exercise. Overjoyed to discover that I was *normal*, I broke down and finally talked to Ofe about the sexual difficulties I had endured for ten years.

"What was his reaction?"

"He was livid. It was the biggest fight we ever had... I tried to explain further and told him I had only learned about arousal a couple of years earlier from Athena and that I had never experienced it myself. In divulging this, he questioned if I had ever had any feelings for him since I had never been aroused by him. I told him it had nothing to do with *him* since I had not experienced arousal with my ex-boyfriend either. He was shocked that I had kept it from him for ten years. He even asked to know when I last desired sex; I explained that I had never desired sex in my life and did not even know what that felt like, and he lashed out and called me a liar. He felt that my lack of sexual desire and inability to orgasm were a reflection of his inadequacy and believed I was lying in order not to hurt him. The whole situation was a nightmare. The more I tried to explain, the deeper I dug myself into a hole since I myself did not really understand my sexual issues."

Edward shook his head.

"It is impossible to explain something you do not fully understand."

"It was a rough time," she smiled.

"How did you get through all of that?"

"It was difficult – we argued whenever we were around each other and things remained like that for nearly a year. At the time, I had just given birth and suffered from postnatal blues which brought back my flashbacks and feelings of depression."

"Was he aware of this?"

"What, the flashbacks?"

"How you were feeling in general."

"I cried a lot when he was not around so initially he had no idea I was depressed. I spoke to him about the flashbacks but because we did not particularly *like* each other much at the time, his response was a bit harsh. He said he did not understand why I continued to allow memories from my past to affect me and that it was getting annoying hearing me talk about flashbacks every day. He basically said I should get over it and move on."

"How did you feel when he said this?"

"It hurt but we were going through a tough time so I did not hold it against him."

Edward chose his words carefully.

"Generally, when people love you they often do not know how to react or act around you when you are hurting, especially when the pain is due to a traumatic experience like sexual abuse. There is a lot of pain, sadness, anger and helplessness on the part of your loved ones and sadly such emotions can sometimes come across as uncaring."

"I never thought about it like that."

He explained further.

"Ofe's comments may have come across as insensitive but they were probably coming from a place of pain or helplessness. Another thing is, experiencing flashbacks or any type of stress as a result of (sexual) trauma is a symptom of PTSD. Unfortunately, some people are of the perception that the individual experiencing PTSD is *choosing* to wallow in self-pity while others view it as a weakness and sadly, it is neither. So being told to get over it and move on is never useful. In *your* case, you had stopped having flashbacks altogether, and when you gave birth to your second child, they returned... this too is normal since in giving birth, your body undergoes tremendous levels of stress. If an individual has ever gone through depression, having a baby can easily bring it on again."

Sexual Healing

A BIG PART OF KEBI'S initial reluctance to go to therapy was due to a lack of information about what it actually entailed. At her twelfth session, she reflected on the impact it had made on her life thus far.

"I have gained more confidence and self-awareness which have both impacted my personal life and my work."

Edward smiled.

"I am glad to hear it has had a positive impact especially on your work, which was the reason why you came here in the first place."

Kebi smiled as he continued.

"I don't think I have asked you this before; how did you get into the sexual health field?"

She sighed.

"I truly believe my abuse drew me into sexual health..."

Edward nodded as she went on.

"After the fight between me and Ofe, I was depressed and since I was still not used to talking about my problems, I wrote lots of dark poems expressing my feelings. I normally never re-read my poems but one night I came across them and read a few. They made me feel sad for myself and incited me to do something about my situation. The next day, I embarked on a journey of self-discovery. I started spending a lot of time in the library reading self-help books and taking notes; and one day, I stumbled across *Cosmopolitan* magazine which gave sex and relationships advice. And from that day on, I bought them every month."

"You found them useful?"

"Absolutely, I learned so much from the magazines and applied everything I learned to my marriage. Sexually, it was not always straightforward since my brain was wired differently as a result of my abuse, but having such information at my fingertips allowed me to begin to see what was physiologically normal (about me) and what was not. For example, I found that I did not have sensitivities in many other spots which were supposed to be sensitive. But that aside, I believe the most important decision I made at the time was to focus on learning more about myself since I was kind of lost and felt a 'disconnect' from the world and from myself. I decided to start paying attention to things that sustained my curiosity (and attention) and in so doing, I discovered my passion for sexual health education. I did some voluntary work in the field and got a job which turned out to be hugely transformative for me since I got to work with people with real-life sexual health problems."

"So it sort of came full circle as you said – your abuse led you into the field."

"It certainly did; even to this day, I learn something new at work every day."

"What would you say is the biggest lesson you have learned from working in sexual health so far?"

Kebi sighed.

"I have learned *so* much professionally but personally, the biggest lessons I have learned stem from a *single* patient."

Edward listened on.

"I was once called in by a female colleague (a doctor) to sit in during a consultation she was having with a female French patient so I could help to translate since I speak French. The reason for the patient's visit was 'pain during sex' and after going through preliminary screening questions, the doctor asked if she had ever been raped. She was initially taken aback by the question but later admitted she had been raped four years earlier. A physical examination and laboratory tests were carried out and the patient was diagnosed with vaginismus, a condition which although I had never heard of, I made every effort to diligently translate as the doctor explained what it was. As I learned on that day, vaginismus was a word used to describe the involuntary tightening of vaginal muscles during penetration."

Edward nodded knowingly as Kebi continued.

"The patient was referred to psychosexual therapy and when she went there for the initial sex therapy consultation, she requested my assistance in translating. During that consultation I got to learn a little more about vaginismus including that it was associated with rape because in trying to prevent penetration during rape, vaginal muscles tightened. Only then did it dawn on me that this was my normal reaction to penetration during sex every single time: my glutes and vaginal muscles tightened involuntarily but I was oblivious to the fact that this was an abnormal reaction to penetration. And because my muscles tightened, sex was always painful."

Edward nodded.

"So that was how you found out..."

"It was..." she smiled, "Isn't it funny how things happen?"

"You must have found the session beneficial."

"Very much so, and in the same consultation the sex therapist said the patient's vaginismus could be reversed, which was music to my ears. She explained that it could be reversed by retraining the vagina to develop a normal response to penetration. She said in order to achieve this, the patient needed to do kegel exercises to relax the pelvic floor muscles and she also needed to use various sized vaginal dilators (which I had never heard of before) to help the vaginal muscles to act more normally over time. She showed her how to use vaginal dilators and explained their usefulness in her recovery. Essentially, I got much-needed sex therapy dropped in my laps that day."

"That's a classic case of being in the right place at the right time," Edward smiled.

"I was extremely fortunate because I cannot fathom how else I would have come across such information without even knowing that I suffered from vaginismus which I had never even heard of before. Anyway, following this, I bought a pack of vaginal dilators (which were like miniature dildos) and the therapist had explained that the patient needed to use them from smallest to biggest over time and that it might hurt a lot at first. I did experience a lot of pain with the smallest-sized one (which was as little as my pinky finger) but in time it got better and they proved extremely useful in completely stopping the involuntary tightening and the pain stopped too. This process also enabled me to understand why I had always experienced vaginal pain whenever I used tampons."

Edward nodded.

"Did you have the same experience with tampons?"

She nodded.

"Always; no matter how small they were, they hurt during insertion, so I was happy to learn why. As for the patient, she was booked in for a few more sex therapy sessions and whenever she attended, instead of opting for the phone translation service she requested for me," Kebi grinned, "And I was secretly grateful for that."

Edward smiled, "Of course."

Kebi went on.

"We also found out the patient had body image issues which she was unaware of until it came up in therapy."

"What issues were these?"

"She was very slim but described herself as fat and said she became obsessed with diet and exercise after her rape."

Edward nodded.

"That's seen quite often in survivors of sexual assault."

"I didn't know this until the therapist explained how it came about."

"What did the therapist say?" Edward asked.

"She explained that when a person is sexually abused they sometimes feel like control is taken *from* them, and that in trying to take back control, the tendency for some people is to focus on 'controlling' the way they look; she said it can sometimes lead to an obsession with diet and exercise and at times cosmetic surgery."

"Absolutely," he agreed, "At times it has the opposite effect with some people becoming depressed and turning to food for comfort resulting in them becoming overweight. On the flip-side, some survivors become body-shamers without even realising it; this is quite common but not always easy to spot since not many people disclose that they were abused."

"So you're saying the person who was raped becomes a bully."

Edward nodded.

"That does happen."

"It reminds me of the saying, *'Hurt people hurt people'*."

Edward agreed.

"At times when a person is hurting, it can be projected onto others in the form of hurtful behaviour," he explained.

Kebi paused.

"I hope I did not project my hurt onto anyone... but I don't think I did since I was kind of quiet."

She paused again and thought of how lucky she was.

"I really like therapy," she said.

Edward smiled.

"Why do you like it?"

"It allows you to see things in a way that might not have been obvious to you before."

"It does give you an objective view," he said, "And it helps you to understand your feelings or actions."

Kebi was curious.

"I wonder about something..."

"Okay?"

"After my abuse, I desperately tried to avoid sexual contact but I am aware that some people instead become sexually promiscuous. Why is there a difference in reactions to sexual abuse and how does sexual promiscuity come about?"

Edward sighed deeply.

"Everyone is different and people are affected by sexual abuse in different ways irrespective of the horrendousness of the abuse. What I mean by this is one person may be groped for two seconds in a train full of passengers and another may be tormented and raped in the manner in which *you* were. Despite the

231

marked difference in the apparent gravity of both assaults, it cannot be predicted which of the victims may become sexually promiscuous and which of them might avoid sex (also known as sexual avoidance). Everyone is affected differently regardless of the type of abuse."

Kebi jotted quickly as he continued to explain.

"After sexual abuse has taken place, a person either exhibits sexually avoidant behaviour or becomes sexually promiscuous.

Being sexually promiscuous means exhibiting compulsive sexual behaviour like having multiple partners, having sex under the influence of drugs or alcohol, or using no protection or contraception. As far as I know, there are no specific physiological reason why a person specifically becomes sexually avoidant or sexually promiscuous after sexual abuse.

But to answer the second part of your question; sexual abuse is about power and control. And as you mentioned earlier, when an individual is sexually abused, they do feel like control is taken from them. For some people, becoming sexually promiscuous is an attempt to reaffirm or regain their control... or to restore what has been taken from them (it is psychological).

Another facet is, after being sexually abused, some people go in search of love and acceptance (because they have been hurt from being sexually abused) but at the same time, they try to protect themselves from getting hurt again by having sex soon after meeting someone (in order to prevent any emotional attachment). However, if they start developing feelings for the individual, they immediately run off to someone else so as not to get too attached; then they end up having multiple partners within a short space of time.

Also, sexual abuse is degrading and humiliating, as you know, and the emotional pain that arises from this is sometimes manifested in the form of sexually-risky behaviour such as having multiple partners, having sex whilst 'high' on drugs and/or using no protection.

Furthermore, after being sexually abused some people feel devalued or worthless and view sex as meaningless. Consequently, they too may begin to engage in 'meaningless sex' as an expression of their feelings of worthlessness. This often goes hand-in-hand with the abuse of drugs and alcohol, in an attempt to numb the pain of feeling worthless and devalued.

And lastly, during an orgasm, there are hormones produced which induce pleasure and also serve as pain relief for pain suffered from an individual's destroyed self-esteem due to sexual abuse. Some people who have been sexually abused crave orgasmic pleasure and in getting that from having lots of sex they may also be benefiting from the feeling of improved self-esteem."

Kebi clarified this as she jotted.

"So having more sex and orgasms can make the person feel better since the hormone gives orgasmic pleasure and improves their self-esteem."

"Correct... but it only provides the person with a momentary feeling of betterment which they continue to pursue by having more sex."

"Oh, so the feeling of improved self-esteem is only temporary?"

"Correct; it does not last long."

Kebi shook her head.

"So, they keep going back again and again for a quick sex fix which is temporary," she sighed, "It really messes one up..."

Edward agreed and continued to explain.

"On the other side of the coin, after sexual abuse has taken place, there may be complete sexual avoidance which is what *you* experienced. And as you already know, sexual avoidance stems from a morbid fear of sex."

Kebi nodded and explained.

"I completely agree; it *was* scary. For many years, I spent several hours each day trying to figure out how to avoid sex and any form of intimacy; it was debilitating living like that especially because Ofe and I lived together.

Thankfully, things started to improve once I learned more about intimacy. I actually learned about self-exploration and sensual self-care from the sex therapist; and self-exploration was ultimately very instrumental in reinstating my bodily sensitivities. It had the additional benefit of allowing me to be able to determine the kind of physical contact I was comfortable with (or not) and this ultimately enabled me to become comfortable with overall romantic physical contact.

With time, it led to an exponential increase in my libido and allowed me to start to feel more in control of my own body. It is something I would highly recommend to anyone with similar sexual issues."

Edward added.

"And you mentioned the dissociation stopped once you addressed the intimacy issues..." he asked.

"Yeah, it stopped way before I started working in sexual health. I believe once I learned how to allow myself to be vulnerable, my exterior protective layer disappeared and the dissociation stopped as a result... but there is something else... I still don't understand how dissociation really comes about."

"Let me explain," Edward said, "Dissociation is the body's way of blocking out the trauma that happened and it occurs prominently in survivors of child abuse because when a person is abused as a child, they have not yet developed any other coping skills. So dissociating (which is withdrawing mentally and physically) becomes the only way the person knows how to react to trauma... does that make sense?"

"I get it now," she nodded, "I guess that is why mine stopped when my brain no longer viewed sex as something traumatic."

"You understand it perfectly," he smiled.

Kebi took some notes and after a long pause, Edward said, "Did you ever dissociate during other stressful events?"

"When I was a child, I dissociated every time I was raped and I believe twice when I was badly beaten by George. I also dissociated when my uncle masturbated on me that evening in his office. But as an adult, I only dissociated during sex. Long after admitting all my sexual difficulties to Ofe, he asked to know what dissociation felt like and when I explained the feeling to him, he was intrigued that a person's brain could actually do that... even *I* still find it mind-blowing."

"What *did* it feel like to dissociate?"

She sighed.

"It was like leaving your body and floating up to the ceiling into a noiseless space and from inside the space, you watched yourself being raped but felt no pain, no sense of physical touch, nothing. And once the rape was over, you snapped back into reality... really weird... but I'm glad it is gone now."

Edward smiled.

"How are things between you and Ofe today?"

237

"Things have been great between us for the last couple of years. Obviously, I was twenty-nine when I *came clean* (to him) about all the sexual issues I had, and I immediately started learning about intimacy and about myself. Learning about myself and starting afresh in sex and intimacy at the age of twenty-nine as a wife and mother of two little kids was exciting but at times, I felt inadequate, insecure and unsure of myself. There were many times when I even felt guilty for having sex and this prevented me from being fully present in the moment.

However, being an avid learner, such obstacles incited me to want to learn more. I listened to audios, watched movies and read tons of books on sex and intimacy and the knowledge I gained has positively impacted my marriage over the last few years."

"You mentioned feeling guilty for having sex with your husband... were you able to overcome these feelings?"

She sighed.

"It took a while – actually it took a long while but I eventually overcame them. I believe my feelings of guilt stemmed from the fact that as a child, everything I knew about sex carried a negative connotation; it caused physical pain, it was a form of punishment, it took place in hiding and was always supposed to be kept a secret. As an adult, when I learned to view it as something positive, it was not easy to shake off the negative beliefs (about sex) that were ingrained in me. Consequently, a lot of the time, I felt guilty for engaging in it.

It was tricky and quite bothersome but to overcome the feelings of guilt, I initially tried meditation (as recommended in a magazine) but that did not work for me. Then I found a book and read a chapter on role-play, tried it once and said goodbye to all my feelings of guilt for good."

"Why do you think role-play helped?"

Kebi paused.

"I wouldn't know the psychological explanation, obviously" she chuckled, "But in lay man's terms, in role-play, pretending to be someone other than myself allowed me to strip away any feelings of guilt (or insecurity) for as long as I wanted and also allowed me to be more daring than I would normally be, since technically it was 'not me' who was partaking in whichever role it was. More so, I had the luxury of being able to separate my actual self from the roles I played but they eventually all became my alter egos. And whenever I felt guilty (or insecure), I conjured the strengths and confidence of any of my alter egos and this helped to eliminate feelings of guilt. As time went on, I progressively experienced a decline in the occurrence of my feelings of guilt during intimacy and no longer felt the need to *hide* behind role-play and alter ego. I had become confident and very self-aware and had the freedom to just be me," she smiled.

"I must say, you have come a very long way," Edward sighed.

"I have and I'm still learning."

"It will only get better - you are on the right path."

He looked at the time.

"Well, this is our final session... How do you feel?" he smiled.

Kebi paused.

"My perception is that, as an infant, I was like a cactus seed planted inside a calabash with no access to sunlight or water, yet expected to flourish. I am fortunate to have survived my childhood abuse since as

I have experienced and learned, its effects can be lifelong and detrimental. Therapy has provided me with insight and as of now, it feels like there are no more missing pieces.

Acknowledgements

Thank you to Oshiokhai, Ebanga, Emoshoriahme and Stephen

Printed in Poland
by Amazon Fulfillment
Poland Sp. z o.o., Wrocław

49477159R00150